PRAISE FOR
DANIEL WOODRELL'S

WOE TO LIVE ON

A *New York Times* Notable Book

"Woodrell joins Douglas C. Jones and the few others whose
novels of western history are mainstream literature.... The
violence is fast and understated and bawdy humor relieves
the story's intensity."

—*Kansas City Star*

"A renegade Western...that celebrates the genre while
bushwhacking its most cherished traditions....Jake Roedel
recites his tale of woe in an improbably rustic idiom, with a
malignant humor and a hip sensibility that are wise ⊦
his years and way ahead of his times."

—*Chicago*

"Woodrell is on the cutting edge of mean...a born ⊦
His style is both brutal and touched with poetry. A
very much his own. Don't miss it."

—*Philadelphia I*

"Woodrell pins it down just right...speaks to the universal cruelty of civil war."

— *St. Louis Post-Dispatch*

"A fine novel....Daniel Woodrell has captured the devastation of war and, more importantly, the twisting of men's minds."

— *United Press International*

"An absolutely brilliant performance."

—David Martin, author of *The Crying Heart Tattoo*

"Like William Kennedy's, Woodrell's prose has a lyrical quality that effectively evokes a sense of place."

— *San Francisco Examiner*

"Woodrell's novel is at once intensely literary and wonderfully cinematic.... *Woe to Live On* is in some ways a celebration of the intertwining of American writing and American speech, of the way, since *Huckleberry Finn* especially (written by Woodrell's fellow Missourian Mark Twain, né Samuel Clemens), American literary prose hears itself in dialogue with transcribed, unschooled, spoken vernacular. But, ironically, when you pull that speech off the written page and throw it up on the screen, the results can be oddly 'literary'—a quality we carefully embraced in the screenplay."

—James Schamus, screenwriter, *Ride with the Devil*

WOE TO LIVE ON

WOE TO
LIVE ON

Daniel Woodrell

Foreword by Ron Rash

BACK BAY BOOKS

LITTLE, BROWN AND COMPANY

New York   Boston   London

Copyright © 1987 by Daniel Woodrell
Foreword copyright © 2012 by Ron Rash
Reading group guide copyright © 2012 by Daniel Woodrell and Little, Brown and Company

Back Bay Books / Little, Brown and Company
Hachette Book Group
1290 Avenue of the Americas, New York, NY 10104
www.hachettebookgroup.com

Originally published in hardcover by Henry Holt and Company, July 1987
First Back Bay paperback edition, June 2012

Back Bay Books is an imprint of Little, Brown and Company. The Back Bay Books name and logo are trademarks of Hachette Book Group, Inc.

The publisher is not responsible for websites (or their content) that are not owned by the publisher.

The Hachette Speakers Bureau provides a wide range of authors for speaking events. To find out more, go to www.hachettespeakersbureau.com or call (866) 376-6591.

A portion of this novel previously appeared in *The Missouri Review*.

Library of Congress Cataloging-in-Publication Data
Woodrell, Daniel.
  Woe to live on / Daniel Woodrell.— 1st Back Bay pbk. ed.
    p. cm.
  "Back Bay Books."
  ISBN 978-0-316-20616-7
  1. United States — History — Civil War, 1861–1865 — Fiction.   I. Title.
  PS3573.O6263W6 2012
  813'.54 — dc23   2011051516

10 9 8 7 6 5

LSC-H

Printed in the United States of America

To all my family, here and now, long gone or still dreamed,
who do, did, or will take stands on every which side of
That Old Mountain, with love and gratitude.

The author wishes to thank the Copernicus Foundation
and the Iowa Writers' Workshop for the assistance
provided by a James A. Michener Fellowship.

FOREWORD

First off, let me say that most American novelists would not have attempted to write this book. They wouldn't have the courage to tell a story where racial epithets are common and, even worse, a major character is a black man who fights for the Confederacy. It would not matter that the offensive language was true to the time period and place or that the black soldier was based on a member of Quantrill's Raiders, a man who can be seen in a 1904 reunion photograph. These are parts of history a good many people would prefer remain unacknowledged, and those people will resent an author for bringing such matters to light.

Readers wishing for a romanticized lament for "the lost cause" will be equally resentful. Woodrell's Confederates are not men of honor who observe the gentlemanly rules of warfare. These soldiers plunder, kill unarmed civilians, and torture their captives. Their mode of warfare is ambush or trickery, even dressing in Union blue to surprise the enemy. The nobility of Southern womanhood is seen in light of a couple rutting on a dirt floor. The only cause the men fight for is vengeance. Their loyalty is to each other, but within the ranks there is hatred and killing. The puritanical, whether on the left or right of the political spectrum, prefer a world without ambiguity or paradox. Woodrell, like all the best artists, is an outlier. His quest in *Woe to Live On* is to render the world as it was, not as we wish it to have been.

"War means fighting, and fighting means killing," Bedford Forrest said. Jake Roedel, the novel's narrator, learns the truth of Forrest's comment all too well. Jake knows that in such times even "mercy has treachery in it." Which brings us to the central question raised in *Woe to Live On*: Is it possible for a man to retain his humanity in an inhuman time, and if not, at least to regain that humanity after a war ends? As Jake puts it, "Our struggle had carried us into a new territory of the soul, where we found new versions of our selves." *Woe to Live On* provides an answer that is neither nihilistic nor sentimental—and is sometimes contradicted in the novel itself—but nevertheless is one that I find satisfying and true to the complexity of the human heart.

There is so much more to praise about this novel—its perfect pacing, the memorable characters, the seamless meshing of history and imagination, but what I admire most in *Woe to Live On* is the language. There is not a moment when the words feel outside the time and place. Words such as *scotched* and *codded* abound. The similes are colorful but they fit the characters' rural backgrounds: "That was clear as cow patties on a snowbank"; "You done did the milkin', might as well lap the cream." The syntax and formality in Jake's telling is true to letters written by Civil War soldiers: "I believed I could not be hit, so absent had I decided myself to be" and "...wondering how many of our dinner companions would share our meals no more."

The horror of war is vividly rendered. This is not a book for the fainthearted. Men kill and are killed, and the reader is spared few details. A scene where a wife's love letter is read aloud to a dying Union soldier is particularly harrowing. But amid the carnage there are moments of lyrical wonder and beauty. One of my favorites is when Jake, hiding out in a barn, observes "the shafts of light spearing down through cracks and illuminating all the grainy debris in the air." It is a moment that brings to mind another soldier, Tolstoy's Prince Andre, who, fallen on the battlefield, sees the sky as though for the first time. Beauty and wonder yet abide in the novel's world. And a belief that, even in the worst of times, we are capable of moments of grace and forgiveness, "that aloneness would not be our fate."

Daniel Woodrell is one of America's best writers, and *Woe to Live On* is one of his finest achievements. The reissue of this novel is cause for celebration.

—Ron Rash

BOOK ONE

Playing war is played out!

— CHARLES R. JENNISON OF
JENNISON'S JAYHAWKERS

BOOK ONE

1

WE RODE ACROSS the hillocks and vales of Missouri, hiding in uniforms of Yankee blue. Our scouts were out left flank and right flank, while Pitt Mackeson and me formed the point. The night had been long and arduous, the horses were lathered to the withers and dust was caking mud to our jackets. We had been aided through the night by busthead whiskey and our breaths blasphemed the scent of early morning spring. Blossoms had begun a cautious bloom on dogwood trees, and grass broke beneath hooves to impart rich, green odor. The Sni-A-Bar flowed to the west, a slight creek more than a river, but a comfort to tongues dried gamy and horses hard rode. We were making our way down the slope to it, through a copse of hickory trees full of housewife squirrels gossiping at our passing, when we saw a wagon halted near the stream.

There was a man holding a hat for his hitched team to drink from, and a woman, a girl in red flannel and a boy who was splashing about at the water's edge, raising mud. The man's voice boomed to scold the boy for this, as he had yet to drink. The language of his bark put him in peril.

"Dutchman," Mackeson said, then spit. "Goddamn lop-eared St. Louis Dutchman." Mackeson was American and had no use for foreigners, and only a little for me. He had eyes that were not set level in his hatchet face, so that he saw you top and bottom in one glance. I watched him close when crowds of guns were banging, and kept him to my front.

"Let us bring Black John up," I said.

I turned in my saddle and raised my right hand above me, waved a circle with it, then pointed ahead. The main group was trailing us by some distance, so we had to pause while Black John brought the boys up. When they were abreast of us the files parted and Black John took one column of blue to the right, and Coleman Younger took the other to the left.

This movement caused some noise. The Dutchman was made alert by the rumble of hooves but had no chance to escape us. We tightened our circle about the wagon, made certain the family was alone, then dismounted.

The family crusted around the Dutchman, not in fear, but to introduce themselves. Our uniforms were a relief to them, for they did not look closely at our mismatched trousers and our hats that had rebel locks trailing below them. This was a common mistake and we took pleasure in prompting it.

Most of the boys couldn't be excited by a single man, so they led their mounts to the stream, renewed their friendship with whiskey and generally tomfooled about near the water. Black John Ambrose, Mackeson, me and a few others confronted the Dutchman. He offered his hand to Black John, whose stiff height, bristly black curls and hard-set face made his leadership plain.

"Wilhelm Schnellenberger," the Dutchman said.

Black John did not extend his own hand, but spit, as Americans are wont to do when confident of their might.

"Are you secesh?" Black John asked, ever so coaxingly. "Are you southern man?"

"Nein," the Dutchman responded. He gradually dropped his hand back to his side. "No secesh. Union man."

I spit, then pawed the glob with my boot.

"Dutchman," Mackeson said. "Lop-eared Dutchman."

"Are you certain you are not at all secesh?" Black John asked once more, his lips split in a manner that might be a grin.

"No, no, no," the apple-headed Dutchman answered. His baffled immigrant eyes wandered among us. He smiled. "No secesh. No secesh. Union man."

The woman, the girl and the boy nodded in agreement, the boy beginning to study our uniforms. He was about four years younger than me and looked to be a smart sprout despite his snubbed nose and loose jaw. I kept a watch on him.

Black John pursed his lips and poised to speak, like a preacher caught breathless between the good news and the bad.

Some of the fellows were in the shallows kicking a stick to and fro, trying to keep it in the air, whiskey to the winner. It was a poetry moment: water, whiskey, no danger, a friendly sun in the sky, larks and laughter.

"Aw, hell," Black John said. "Stretch his neck. And be sharp about it."

The woman had some American, and the Dutchman had

enough anyway, for when she flung her arms about him wailing, he sunk to his knees. His head lolled back on his neck and his face went white. He began mumbling about his god, and I was thinking how his god must've missed the boat from Hamburg, for he was not near handy enough to be of use in this land.

Mackeson goaded me. "What's he babblin'?"

"He is praying to Abe Lincoln," I answered.

A rope was needed. Coleman Younger had a good one but would not lend it as it was new, so we used mine. Mackeson formed it into a noose with seven coils rather than thirteen, for he had no inclination to bring bad luck onto himself. Thirteen is proper, though, and some things ought to be done right. I raised this issue.

"You do it then, Dutchy," Mackeson said, tossing the seven-coiled rope to me. "Bad luck'll not change your course anyhow."

The rope burned between my fingers as I worked to make the Dutchman's end a proper one. The situation had sunk in on the family and they had become dull. The Dutchman saw something in me and began to speak. He leaned toward me and wiggle-waggled in that alien tongue of ours. I acted put upon by having thus to illustrate my skill in oddball dialects, lest I be watched for signs of pride in the use of my parents' language.

"We care nothing for the war," the Dutchman said. He had lost his hysterics for the moment and seemed nearly sensible. I respected that, but fitted the noose with thirteen coils around his neck. "We are for Utah Territory. Utah. This is not a war in Utah, we learn."

"This war is everywhere," I said.

"I am no Negro-stealer. I am barrel maker."

"You are Union."

"*Nein.* I am for Utah Territory."

I gave the long end of the rope to Mackeson, as I knew he wanted it. He threw it high up over a cottonwood branch, then tied it to the trunk.

Jack Bull Chiles was standing between Mackeson and the water; and as he was my near brother, raised on the same bit of earth, he hustled the Dutchman toward the wagon for me. Some of the other boys joined him, and they lifted the center of attention to the seat of the wagon, startling the team, and setting off screeches of metal on wood, mules and women.

I stepped back from the wagon's path, then turned to Black John.

"He says he is not a Union man," I told him. I was flat with my voice, giving the comment no more weight than a remark on the weather. "He was codded by our costumes."

"Sure he says that," Mackeson said. "Dutchman don't mean 'fool.'"

"Now he says he is sympathetic to our cause, does he?" Black John said. He was remounted and others were following suit. "Well, he should've hung by his convictions rather than live by the lie." Black John swelled himself with a heavy breath, then nodded to Mackeson. "He's just a goddamn Dutchman anyhow, and I don't much care."

Mackeson winked meanly at Schnellenberger, then stepped past him and slapped the mules on the rump.

The immigrant swung, and not summer-evening peaceful, but frantic.

"One less Dutchman," Coleman Younger said.

They all watched me, as they always did when wrong-hearted Dutchmen were converted by us. They were watching me even as they faced away, or giggled. Such an audience compelled me to act, so I mounted my big bay slowly, elaborately cool about the affair.

The woman was grieved beyond utterance, her eyes wide and her mouth open and trembling, as if she would scream but could not. The little girl was curled in behind *Mutter's* big skirts, whimpering.

The boy I watched, as I'd pegged him for smart. With his hands hanging limp at his sides he walked beneath his father's dancing boots, then gave a cry and made a move to loosen the rope about the cottonwood trunk. He was close to fourteen and still foreign to his toes.

I gave no warning but the cocking of my Navy Colt and booked the boy passage with his father. He did not turn, and the ball tore him between the blades. His death was instant.

My face was profound, I hoped, when I faced Black John.

"Pups make hounds," I said. "And there are hounds enough."

Black John nodded, then said solemnly, "Jake Roedel, you are a rare Dutchman."

Pitt Mackeson glared at me wrinkle-nosed, as if I were something hogs had vomited.

"Did you see that?" he asked. "Shot the boy in the back! Couldn't shoot him face-to-face. Goddamn Dutchman! Why'd you back-shoot him?"

"I am tender toward boys," I said. "But I would put a ball in your face, Mackeson, should affairs so dictate."

There was a silence that gave off steam, then Black John repeated himself on the sort of Dutchman I was and we rode away in the silence of the family's pain.

Jack Bull sidled his blue-black mount next to mine and we rode together. My near brother had a squared forehead and a narrow chin and manly brown eyes atop an uncrushed nose. The effect was pleasing to most folks. His dark hair had length, and his long, lean body was capable of quickness, but only after careful thought.

"You want to watch that man," he said quietly.

I was positioned so that Pitt Mackeson's sweat-targeted blades were ever visible to me. He seemed to know it and took great interest in what he had just ridden past.

"I believe I can," I said. "He needs hurting."

"Aw," Jack Bull said. "You expect too much of him. He is dumb and mean and snaky, but he is a good Yankee-killer." Jack Bull had, by virtue of the station to which he'd been born, an air of educated understanding about him. "You must admit that he is a fine Yankee-killer."

"He is a good killer, Jack Bull. And this season he kills Yankees."

"Comrades can be made of less," he responded. "Keep it in mind."

I had many comrades who were made of nothing but the same. I saw the truth of it and would not squawk that they were not made of more.

Our course took us into the bottoms of the Blackwater River. The land was moist there, and the roads were heavy.

We were unmilitary in our formation but watchful of everything.

Near on to noon we came to a small farm and halted. We scanned the scene and saw nothing of threat in it.

"Some of you boys go make us known," Black John commanded. Cave Wyatt, Riley Crawford, Bill House and Silas Mills rode directly to the door and hailed the inhabitants.

An old woman soon came onto the porch. Her dress was gray and thick and smudged, and her boots carried mud.

"Who is it?" she asked.

Most of the country men in this county were loyal to the South and necessary to us, so rough tactics were held back until sympathy had a chance to win.

"Why, we are southern men," Cave said. "And hungry."

"You don't look like southern men," the old woman said back. "How do I know?"

Riley Crawford was from this county, and being not over sixteen he had a trustworthy face. Jayhawkers had tortured his father with devilish rope tricks and, thus left fatherless, Riley had grown into a killer young.

He spoke. "Woman, my name is Crawford. One of the Six-Point Creek Crawfords—do you know me?"

The woman stomped the mud from her boots on the planks of the porch, then nodded.

"I knew the father," she said. "Him and plenty more. Come on and eat as what we have."

We went into the yard and dismounted. The nips of whiskey had built us all appetites, so we were lazy about posting pickets. This was often the case.

We numbered twenty-one men. The woman, who had the name of Clark, was kept hopping. She brought us trays of biscuits and molasses, coffee and milk.

I went to the kitchen to assist her, as I had no vanity about cooking work.

"Are you alone here?" I asked her.

Her face was round and pleasant, but aged by the times. Skin sagged at her throat, yet there was tightness about the eyes.

"Yes," she said. Then, jolted by the thought of her lie, "No. My man is at Arkansas with Shelby. My son is in the barn."

"Is he grown?"

"He was," she said. "He gave up a leg at Wilson's Creek. I keep him hid away." She grabbed a biscuit tray and turned from me. "Jayhawkers have been about here. They would kill him."

"He should come with us."

"No," she said, and shook her head. "He won't fight. He is done with that."

In the front room I ate with the men, all squatted about the floor. Our many pistols scraped the floorboards and made sitting thus a skill, but no complaints were ever made of that.

I hunkered next to Jack Bull as usual, and Arch Clay, Bill House and Cave, who looked at me from his plate and said, "You are an interestin' foreigner, Jake."

"Why is that?" I asked amiably, as Cave often had me on with jokes.

He wiped a molasses drool from his brown beard and

answered, "Because you are loyal to here and not there. Uncommon."

My eyes met Jack Bull's, then he shrugged and ate on, looking down.

Soon I had eaten my fill. I tapped Jack Bull on the arm and bid him come with me.

"Where?"

"The barn. There is a son hiding out in the barn."

The barn had been part burned down, and only one half stood strongly. Some hay was put by there, but little else.

"Halloo inside," Jack Bull called as we entered. "We are friends, Clark. Show yourself."

From our backs came some sniggering in a thin tone that was eerie. We turned toward it and instinct had our hands on our pistols.

The sniggering continued while we saw from where it came. A smallish man lay on a hay pile behind the door, a shotgun at his side. The roof half that was gone from flame let in plenty of light. But there was an unwell scent to the room.

"Bushwhackers," Clark said between sniggers. "I could've killed you both." His hand tapped the shotgun. "But it ain't even loaded."

"No need of that," I said. "We are friends."

"You s'pose so, do you?" Clark asked. "I don't."

His left leg was absent from near the hip down. A red neckerchief was tied to the stump. He looked a hard ride beyond Grim.

"You were at Wilson's Creek," I said. "Who with?"

"Why, General Price," Clark said. He had blue eyes. "The fat glory-hound rebel himself."

Jack Bull hunkered down and pointed at the stump. "Didn't see that one coming, eh?"

This set Clark to sniggering again with such force that it ended in coughs. Breathing was a tussle. His face reddened.

"I saw it comin'. I see *everything*. Don't think I don't. I saw it rollin' past little piles of kindlin' stuff that I once knew by name. I watched it roll right up to me."

Jack Bull laughed and spit, then courteously calmed. "You weren't *too* quick with both legs, were you?"

"I was plenty quick." Clark stopped with the mirth and looked dour. "Don't you believe I wasn't. But nature borned me smart and that changes things."

In that war one-eyed, one-eared, two-stumped warriors were not uncommon, so Clark's pathetic qualities failed to be as touching as he supposed.

"General Price is a good man," I said. "Would you have us fetch you something to eat?"

"I have a mother for that," Clark said. "I don't eat anyway. I'm tryin' somethin' different."

Jack Bull still squatted, staring at the air where the leg once grew, chewing a straw end as he contemplated something. Soon he pointed a finger at the stump and slowly spoke: "Now, tell me this, Clark. If you were plenty quick and saw it coming, how could you not avoid the cannonball?"

Clark tossed his head back deeper in the hay, and gazed up at the sun through the half roof.

"It looked like good luck. There was arms in trees and

rebels dropped in sections all about." He breathed whistly, like a sick bird might sing. "We never been well off here. Never. We never even owned so much as a single spavined nigger. Oh, mister—there was neighbors gone to Kingdom all around me."

"Wilson's Creek *was* a hot one, wasn't it?" Jack Bull said. He then looked at me. "Arch and Cole were in it. They describe it like that. Hot."

"Yes," I said. Then, "But, Clark—your leg."

"Aw," he said and part pulled himself up. "I wanted my foot broke so I could head home. The damned little cannonball was goin' slower'n a fevered rabbit. Do you respect me? I was there, and I put my foot out just hopin' for a bone to snap."

"Why, you are a fool," I said. "A cannonball will rip your leg right—"

"Ho, ho, ho," went Clark, then followed it up with more of those eerie sniggers. The sound wafted eloquently about the barn and required no accompaniment of further conversation.

Experience had prepared me for all manner of ridiculous misfortune befalling a man. Gopher holes killed governors and tick bites emptied neighborhoods. But this man Clark's misfortune had been to be who he was and think himself smart in the wrong era for delusions.

"Well, now," Jack Bull said as he stood, no longer interested. "Perilous times do not make us all stronger. It is sad to see."

I stared down at Clark, a cripple by bad choice, and felt certain he would not last long, as death offers so many opportunities to nitwits.

"You will be killed," I said to him. "Jayhawkers or militia, someone or the other will stop here and kill you."

"Aw, they been here already and burned the barn. I wouldn't even move to put it out. Ma done it." He lay down again, his memories no doubt on the attack back behind his blank face. "As likely you boys will kill me. I don't much care."

This comment exhausted Jack Bull's forbearance, as he had seen too many good men pass over the river who did not care for the trip.

"You want to die, do you?" Jack Bull's voice was taut and his expression was unlovely. He could be mean. I knew this. "Perhaps you would choose to die now." He pulled a pistol and held it aimed down. "I have considerable experience in the killing line, Clark. I could do you a fair job of it, this minute."

Clark pondered this with wretched concentration showing in his face, then said, "No. No. Ma has her heart set on me livin'."

"Are you sure of that?" Jack Bull asked. "I am here and now and loaded."

After a few more of those sick songbird breaths, Clark said, "I don't believe so. I think I'll wait on it."

Jack Bull slowly holstered his pistol and we walked to the door. There he paused and turned to Clark.

"Your mother is a fine enough woman. You might help her some, don't you think? You get yourself a stick to lean on and you could limp around a good bit."

"Uh-huh," Clark said. "That could be next." He was still flat on his back and staring up at the vastness. "That could be the very next thing."

2

W HEN EVENING HAD been thrown over us, we were camped at a woods on a farm owned by a man named Sorrells. A brook sang near us, and our pickets had a good view from the mound we occupied. Fires were lit, as we knew the militia feared to travel in this country by night. We ruled the dark roads.

Arch Clay had produced his deck of cards and was trying to teach gambling games to the Hudspeth brothers. Neither of them had turned seventeen and they came of good family, so they possessed no skills in idolatrous pastimes. I did not join them, as I had no spirit for games.

"Now what have you?" Arch asked. Arch was a runtish, dandified man who killed more jollily than I found well mannered. He was Black John's closest friend and sole confidant.

"Two of these here," Babe Hudspeth said, holding his cards aloft toward the light. "The black-hearted ones—is that good?"

"We call them 'spades,'" Arch instructed. "And you?" he asked of Ray Hudspeth.

"Three," Ray said. He was beaming from the ease with

which he had become a successful gambler. "All puppies' feet—do I win the money?"

"Puppies' feet!" Arch exclaimed. He looked at me sourly, though I was no more than one year senior to the brothers. "Can you fathom that? Puppies' feet!" He threw his cards onto the blanket. "Them's clubs, you damned children. No more gamblin' for me. I can't enjoy it like this."

The Hudspeths shared glances, then Babe said, "Just who do you think you're damning, Clay?"

Arch was half-sized on either of the boys but older and more certain.

"Did I hurt your feelings, son?"

"Well," Babe answered, not quite convinced of how he should feel. "It was rude of you."

"Ha," Arch snorted, and lay back on the blanket, tipping his hat forward across his eyes. "That's the least bad I've been for years. It was good of you children to note it for me. Makes me feel all warm and Christian."

I left the Hudspeths to their own thoughts and wandered to join another group of comrades. I generally whittled something useless and strolled of an evening. It relaxed me and made me feel at home.

I joined Jack Bull Chiles, Coleman Younger and Pitt Mackeson on the dark ground beneath a tall oak tree. Cole regarded me intensely, watching as I sat and scraped at a branch. His eyes did not leave me when he thrust a whiskey bottle forward.

I sheathed my knife, then accepted the bottle. I appreciated his generosity to the measure of a quarter pint on the first swallow.

"Do not think you are a good man," Coleman Younger said. "The thought will spoil you."

"I am a southern man," I said. "And that is as good as any man that lived 'til he died."

Coleman Younger was reddish in skin and hair, with the temperament that is wed to that hue, and girth and grit enough to back it up.

"You are a southern man—that is proven," he said. "But a rare one."

For Coleman Younger to speak of me so set a glow in me that whiskey could not match, nor doubt extinguish. It was for this that I searched, communion and levelness with people who were not mine by birth, but mine for the taking.

"Oh, yes, Roedel," Mackeson said. "You are proven to be a southern man who eats kraut and kills boys from the back."

"If the boy had freed the rope, the hanging would've been scotched and required doing over," I said.

"Judas worked quick, too," said Pitt Mackeson.

Cole slowly savored a swallow of inspirational popskull, then said, "You did right. Dead from the front is no more dead than from the back. It is a question of opportunity."

"So is chicken stealin'," Mackeson said. His lopsided face viewed me from my topknot to my toes in a steady glance.

"Do you wish you had more often spoken to your great-grandfather, Mackeson?" I asked. "Tell me."

My arms ached already from the thought of digging his eternal home, for I was thinking he would soon be in it.

"How could I wish that, Dutchy? I never even knew him." Mackeson was confused. "He was gone years before I was borned."

I slid my hand toward my belly gun, and hunched over to shade the move.

"Well, your introduction to him may be close at hand if you so wish."

"Now, none of that," Coleman Younger said. His person and voice had authority. "Jake did right. And *that* is *that*. We are comrades."

"I hear you sayin' it," Mackeson replied. He stood and looked down on me, then began to walk off. "I've heard many a thing said that wasn't so, too." He left us then.

"I'm telling you, Jake," Jack Bull said, "you want to watch that man."

The whiskey bottle was once more in my hand, so I took a share of it.

"Perhaps I should put him where he'll not need so much watching," I suggested.

"Naw, naw," Cole said. "In a hot place Pitt is a good man to have with you."

"I hear you saying it," I answered.

We drank then, on into full dark and hooty-owl time, after which the three of us slept, our bedrolls not a rifle's length apart. Coleman Younger was not a regular part of our band, and soon he left us, but for that one brief period he was my comrade.

In the morning we shed our blue sheep's clothing. Our border shirts came out of satchels and onto our backs. We preferred this means of dress, for it was more flat-out and honest. The shirts were large, with pistol pockets, and usually colored red or dun. Many had been embroidered with ornate stitching by loving women some were blessed enough to have.

Mine was plain, but well broken in. I can think of no more chilling a sight than that of myself, all astride my big bay horse, with six or eight pistols dangling from my saddle, my rebel locks aloft on the breeze and a whoopish yell on my lips.

When my awful costumery was multiplied by that of my comrades, we stopped faint hearts just by our mode of dread stylishness.

That morning we dawdled about camp more than usual. Black John squatted up to an oak trunk and consulted long with Press Welch, a rider from George Clyde's group. We often linked up with Clyde, or Quantrill, or Poole, Jarrett and Thrailkill. By having many captains we kept our bands small for easy hiding, but we could call all together in a few days' time.

After Press Welch departed, Black John pinched his cheeks together and looked down, lost in some manner of stern thought. He was older than most of us and had lived in Kansas. When being formal he called us the First Kansas Irregulars, which I never heard anyone echo except in his presence. His head was a riot of black tangling hair on the skull and cheeks both. Long-faced, he had a hollowed look brought on by a steady ration of hard days.

"Men..." he finally spoke, raising himself from the ground. "Men, there is work to be done." His voice was low and thick and Baptist-certain that what it spoke was right. "Hampton Eads and seven other of our comrades were took by the militia out of Warrensburg. You had friends among them."

This was not a rare sort of news, but we began to pay attention. Something would be done.

Black John spread his arms wide as if to calm us, although we were yet subdued. "They are all murdered."

Oaths were uttered at this, and Black John commanded us to mount. This we quickly did, and soon we were afield, feeling wolfish, searching for victims.

They were in good supply.

We made trash of men and places. At Sweet Springs we found the houses of two Unionists who had tried to waylay Cave Wyatt when he had visited his mother there. Both men were unaware of us and smug—but not for long. Cave put amens to their miserable existences after delivering unto them a knotty sermon. Their homes became beacons.

Several of the boys were from this neighborhood and had scores to settle. A man called Schmidt thought a fox was in his henhouse but encountered a larger thief than he was prepared for. His end was merciful, as he was a good runner and nearly made the woods.

Following Davis Creek we traveled north by west, swooping on known Union properties and persons. Word of our presence traveled fast, and by midday all we found were empty houses to destroy. Here and there we confiscated silverware or jewelry that had fallen into the wrong hands. But there was not much of it.

Our devotion to revenge began to dull after that, and we yearned to ambush some food and plenty of it.

Turner Rawls had family on the creek, so we stopped in

there for dinner. All horses but two were secreted in a ravine behind the house. Turner's father had been shot in Warrensburg for buying more lead than one man could need, and his two brothers were somewhere in Arkansas with Price. This made him the only protector of his mother and two sisters. He was tender in attitude when about them, a level of temperament he had never before displayed. It made me fonder of him.

The women set us a fine table: chicken fried the way mothers do it, and ham with sweet potatoes, biscuits and coffee. I was zealous about the ham and sweet potatoes, and soon had my fill. Having my fill made me sleepy, so I went onto the porch. It was a fine, sunny day and I decided to count the nailheads in the porch ceiling. To do this I lay on my back, but quickly I lost the count.

Sneezing horses awakened me. I sat up, but they were there: Four militiamen stared at me from behind carbines. A good distance off there was a larger gaggle of bluebellies.

The house had gone silent.

"Where's the other, you devil?" asked one of the militia. He had puppy cheeks and foam at the mouth. He gestured at the two horses we had left out front. "Speak up and maybe you'll live yet."

This brought haw-haws from his brethren, who were a pink-jowled lot of bad citizens.

My comfort was diminished. The full gullet made me feel slow and perhaps stupid.

"Get his guns," the foamy man said. One of the others acted as if he would come forward to disarm me, but hesitated. "Halloo inside! Come out and show your parole or surrender."

Southern men who would not fight could post parole bonds to walk about with a little freedom. I had no parole, and I was armed, as no paroled man could be.

The main body was now coming forward, and a quick scout told me there was fifty or more of them. The numbers were not favorable.

"I am alone," I said. "That's my daddy's house. He was shot off it three days back."

"He lies," said a shrewd militia. "Let's parole him to Jesus, and right now."

I was still seated, and that saved me. The house exploded in the militia's faces, and four saddles were instantly unburdened. I pulled to my knees and grabbed the reins of our two horses and began to run to the rear of the house.

"Get in here!" voices called to me, but I knew we needed the horses, though neither was mine.

My course was changed when the troop of militia opened up on me. I heard the enchanting whack of bullet on meat. Both horses screamed and spasmed, one dropping dead while the other spun in a tight agonized whirl, the rear legs useless.

The bullets were coming in gangs, as I was a lonely target. The little finger on my left hand, a fairly useless digit, was cleaved from me. I saw it land pink and limp in the dust of the chicken pen but made no move to regain it.

Two more strides put me in the house.

At every window there were guns pointing out. Black John stood at the front one, a man cool and plausible.

The women were on the floor and not in the right spirit for the adventure that had befallen them. Turner Rawls crouched nearby his family, pistol pulled, as if the center of the floor was his last stand.

"Do you kill women?" Black John called out the window. "There are women in here!"

The militia was on three sides of us now, and from the house to the wooded ravine and horses there was a clear patch of fifty yards.

Running it would be hot.

"You know we don't," came back a bossy honk of a Yankee voice. You might fight a voice like that for any small reason, let alone for invading your neighborhood. "Send them out now and they'll be safe passaged!"

A bone-and-pulp nubbin was all of my finger I had left. My blood spotted the floor and walls. Someone told me I was hit, as if I might have overlooked it myself. I took a rag and wound it firm about the aching nubbin. The pain was shrill enough, but the idea of a finger of mine twitching about, lost in chicken-pecked dust, was more terrible.

"Please, Ma, you got to go," Turner Rawls was pleading.

Ma Rawls looked at him somewhat berserkly, then waved a hand in his face.

"We're goin', son," she said. "You best believe we're goin'. There ain't no way we're *not* goin'."

She and the sisters were soon on the porch. We watched as they walked to the militia. There was a pinch of dignity to their stride but a peck of pace to it.

Once the courtesies were out of the way, the militia sent a hurricane of bullets to batter the house. We stayed low and returned the weather as best we could.

Holes began to be chewed through the thin planks, and splinters flew about plenty.

It was not a situation we had wanted for ourselves.

"We cain't hold them from here," Turner Rawls said. He reflected the desperation many of us were beginning to feel—mouth agape, skin paled, features gorged with concern.

Black John was still cool, as always, but he was well known to be sane only in a peculiar way.

"Stand fast, boys," he said. "We'll kill them yet."

Just as he spoke, several mounted men charged the house, tossing torches at the roof. They had a ferocious covering fire but we hit two of the riders, one flopping loose to the ground the lovely way they do when dead.

Flames could soon be smelled and heard on the roof and side porch. None of us cared at all for the crispy end that portended. Smoke had to be wrestled for a breath of air.

"We'll just have to take what chances we have runnin'," said Coleman Younger.

"They'll riddle us down! They'll riddle us down!" a panicky Hudspeth spoke. "Shit, there ain't so much as a stump out there for cover."

A general pandemonium now broke out. We were all on our stomachs, smoke-blind, trying to find a place to go. Starke Helms and a boy called Lawson crawled under a bed. They were quivering from the odds.

The flames began licking at us like a mad dog's tongue through a porch rail.

Black John stood, then kicked at the bed.

"Come on, men!" he shouted. "Let's go get it!"

"No!" said a voice from beneath the four-poster. I don't know which man said it. "We're all gonna die out there! We'll die certain out there!"

"This is no time for debate," Black John howled, then booted out the back door and put his long legs to use. We all followed except for the two men under the bed. Their timidity would cost them.

We popped shots as we ran, hopeless, desperate cries coming from us. There was no chance to aim and our bullets whizzed off in all haphazard directions. Bill House went down clutching his knee, and the ground was monstrous pecked by the militia fire. Pete Kinney reached back for House only to have his head exploded. Lane, Martin and Woods also fell, maybe not dead but as good as.

I could run with only so much care and I applied it all to myself.

Several of us were hurting but moving when we reached the woods. Turner Rawls had a hole in the cheek and much blood running from his mouth. Jack Bull Chiles was unhurt and I gained his side as we scrambled pell-mell down the wooded ravine to our horses.

We hit the downslope of woods with such energy that some were injured from not being able to dodge trees. It was tricky that way, and I popped my noggin on a sly branch myself. A blood egg grew above my eye and there was some agony.

Jack Bull put an arm about me and led me to my mount. We were quickly in the saddle, flinging shots at the militia, who were coming into the ravine after us.

"Split up!" Black John shouted. "We'll meet at The Place."

The Place was McCorkle's farm, which was designated as such for occasions of just this sort.

The militia came on the trot down the slope, crowding us. Those of us who would turned and exchanged fire with them, reminding them thusly of the frailty of the human vessel.

But they came on, bold from the advantage they held. The fighting became close in, as there was no good path for us to flee along. Carbines banged about us and our pistols barked back, horses screamed with panic and a chorus of voices cried, "This way, men!" or "Down there, boy!" or "I got one!"

As we made our way into the woods, men gained on us. A big Yank on a black horse mis-aimed a round, then began to club his carbine at me, but the branches were so bunched that he was ineffective with his blows. My aching head was a mirage on my shoulders; it was no longer much of an instrument, but I managed to see him and shoot. The ball scored him somewhere. He gasped and gave up on me.

My horse, Old Fog, a trusty beast, somehow followed Jack Bull's blue-black Valiant. Gunfire and cries and murders went on, but we made it to a field of dry stumps and scrub oak. We covered some ground, you might say—quickly.

When distance enough had been achieved, some objectivity reentered our thoughts and we halted to see who we were and how bad off.

Jack Bull Chiles was still unhurt, Riley Crawford's foot was bloodied but he said it was trivial, my head was not quite real but I lived, and Babe Hudspeth had a significant gash in his forehead. Turner Rawls looked anxious from blood loss but he was a sturdy-made man.

This, then, was our group.

"Where is my brother?" young Hudspeth asked. The crimson flow ran in a rivulet down the bridge of his nose, encircling, but not entering, his eyes. "Did you see my brother?"

"Bock Yawn," Turner told him. Some teeth had been pulled rudely by the round through his cheek, and air escaped from two holes now so that his words were low-note riddles rather than precise. "Woof im. Alibe."

Staring across the field through which we had passed, Jack Bull kept watch for pursuit. There seemed to be none.

"That was sure enough hot," he said, his voice an octave or two more jaunty than I felt. "I think I killed a runt. They left us hurting—that's certain."

The agony of my head and forlorn finger had me in a state that could be called fearless. Safety was not in my thoughts, but relief was, and death seemed at that moment to be a remedy, although it was one I would wait for others to dose out.

The blood egg on my brow throbbed and throbbed as if it might crack open to reveal a condor.

"Goddamn murderin' militia!" Riley Crawford said. "I'll kill ten men for this wound and a thousand if I'm crippled!"

Hudspeth had dismounted and was rubbing mud on his gash. Turner was in the saddle but slumped over. I was more or less the same.

"We'd best be on the move," Jack Bull said.

When Hudspeth was remounted, we followed my near brother. He chose good routes and by evening we were at a farm pond somewhere deep in Lafayette County, moaning a bit, but mostly somber, wondering how many of our dinner companions would share our meals no more.

3

A NIGHT'S REST WENT a long way toward curing me. But the loss of my finger made me cry. Tears just ran over my face. I don't know why. The digit was not of much consequence to my life, but I guess I had been more fond of the useless little thing than I knew. The pain was there but steady, and my head was a kind of caricature I would live with.

Food was our main requirement. At a small house well off any roads, we stopped. Riley Crawford went forward to test the trustworthiness of his youthful visage once more. An old man with a shiny skull came slyly around the side of the house. He carried a shotgun, then put it on Riley but went lackadaisical when their eyes met.

"What do you want, you secesh bastard?"

"Food, sir."

"Eat dirt," the stingy grouch spoke.

"Please don't shoot me," Riley responded. He did an excellent mimic of a pitiful waif. "I am but a boy far from home."

The old man stared and stared, then shook his head.

"I'll not feed you, but I'll not shoot you either. Now get on out of here."

"That is too kind of you," Riley said. His pistol flushed up from his holster faster than a grouse and he pegged the old tightwad twice in the head. The old man never saw what happened to him, but went down, bloody and extinct, victimized by a dull perspective on youths.

We entered the man's home quickly. It was but a shack; you would not have thought it worth dying over. Out the back window I observed an old granny deer-hopping across a field, her youthful bounce somehow regained. I made no mention of it.

We filled burlap bags with such provisions as we found. No coffee, but some hardtack, back bacon and pickled corn.

To linger would have been to overtest the fates, so we set fire to the dry wood of the house, and rode on to picnic in some more idyllic spot.

Hog paths became our highway. We stuck to backwoods routes and eased toward McCorkle's. It was several miles distant. There was a shyness to our passing, for Turner was poorly and confrontations of no appeal to us.

All we sought was the safety of our comrades.

Jack Bull and I conversed as we traveled.

"This is fine land," I said.

"It is. It is," he answered. "When untroubled. Which it has never been."

"It may someday be," I said, for I was yet an immigrant in a few ways, optimism being one.

"Nah. Nah, we are not made that way. If the Lord called a barn dance, I would halt the old Fiddler and draw Him into conversation. I would ask Him what is in store for us. His answer would surely be the common one—'Why, trouble, my son. As usual.'"

Bleakness had never been Jack Bull's way, but experience was instructing him thus.

"It is not the *what*," I said, "but the *why* that I would ask Him of."

This set Jack Bull to chuckling, as if I were a fool or a subtle wit.

"That is asking too much," he said. "Way too much. Of Him or anyone else."

It *was* a fine region, though. The water was clear and clean and generally nearby. The hills pleased the eye but were not steep enough to daunt one. The dirt was deep and rich, with a scent you would admire in a gravy, and the meadows had a lushness that made you yearn to be a grazing beast. Game was abundant to the point of pestiness, and the forests provided all the building materials an empire could require.

It was altogether a land I was thankful to be in.

That is, but for the trouble.

Distancing ourselves from the turmoil replenished our swagger. We became more usual as the day aged. Except for Turner Rawls, whose distress was spellbinding to him.

There was little we could do to comfort him, but we kept him in the saddle and moving.

When we were yet some miles short of our destination,

the day turned surly on us. A black puddle of storm rallied on the horizon. The wind picked up and on its breeze we smelled bad tidings. A storm was but a storm, but out of doors it was miserable.

We watched it charge down on us.

Babe Hudspeth spoke up with a suggestion.

"I believe, if I ain't lost, that one mile over we'll find Mr. Daily's house. I've stopped there before. I know I ain't lost. It's over there. He is a southern man and generous."

As we paused to think this over, Turner launched into some sort of speech, but his pronunciation was now so double-holed and half scabbed that only a scholar could unscramble it. By his gestures it seemed that he was saying he was entirely in favor of visiting Mr. Daily.

So there we went.

After some initial caution Daily admitted us to his home. He had a farm that might have been prosperous once but now was little more than a weeded-over hideout. Working in the fields was too dangerous when so many bad people were about.

"You are welcome," Daily said. He was a fair chunk of man with cropped gray hair and bowed legs. He had a wife edging around and two daughters who were still in the tyke stage. "Who have you boys worked on lately? I heard Sweet Springs was shot up some."

"We were in on that," Jack Bull said. "They will remember us for it, too."

"Aha," went Daily. He seemed proud of us. "I was told you killed Schmidt and Veale and Ogilvy—is it so?"

Jack Bull shrugged and turned to me.

"Did we?" he asked. "I know we killed some men. I know that."

"Schmidt was one," I said. "He was the runner." Dutch deaths always etched clear in my memory. "And it seems that the men Cave Wyatt tended to were Veale and Ogilvy."

"Wyatt," said Daily. "Yes, Cave Wyatt. That's a good family over there. The Wyatts." He nodded several times. "A fine family."

Riley's foot was not wounded much, really, so he put our horses in the barn. Turner had already laid himself out on the floor and was having fevery dreams while the rest of us men watched the heavens crack down on weak limbs and loosely laid fence rails. Frail buds were whisked into a mangle by the wind. It was a dark, scouring, wet and majestic eruption, and it made one feel tiny and squashable.

The universe sometimes makes war seem a mere chigger in comparison, but that is in no way soothing to one who has the itch.

Our host saw to it that we were fed. It was not much, squirrel with biscuits and thin pan gravy. Nonetheless we ate it all and deluged Mrs. Daily with compliments.

She was a nervous, unjoyful woman, though, and did not seem to believe us or care. Perhaps joy did not come her way much of late, as the Happy Train of Life had long been derailed in these parts.

It grew dark and soon was bedtime but Daily seemed fond of our company. Turner drank milk and dreamed hot, mumbly dramas by turns, while we all sat about being windy. The tykes slept off away from us, and when the mother was gone Daily pulled out a jug of good cheer.

We began to pass it and blow harder at one another. Daily told how he had once been to New Orleans and met a woman there who hadn't a hair left on her; she had shaved herself complete. There was a peeled appleness to her. This fascinated him and he spoke of it as you would of a dog that sang, and well.

"That is disgusting," Babe Hudspeth said, although he laughed. "But why would she do it, anyhow?"

Jack Bull once again exhibited his education.

"Why, to set one whore apart from another, Babe. It is a harlot's brand of showmanship."

Daily bobbed his head and drank. "It is a damned fine show, too. I could see it again and still be interested."

I reckon we laughed at this, for Mrs. Daily came in and snatched up the jug. She had plenty of hair herself and it was in glum disarray.

"I will not have you gettin' drunk in my home," she said. "I am a Baptist and drunkenness is not something I will tolerate."

This embarrassed Daily. He slumped for a moment, then stood and snatched back the jug. "I am not drunk," he told her. "I am entertaining our company."

She put her hands on her hips in that wet-hen way they have.

"You are drunk, Claude. It is ever so plain to me that you are drunk."

"Nah," he bleated. He bent and set the jug in the middle

of the floor. "Nah, I'm not drunk, Sal. I'm barely happy and not drunk at all—could a drunk man do this?"

Several feet of bare planking surrounded the jug, and Daily began to dance on the open floor. He jigged closer and closer to the jug, kicking at it, his toes whiskering past, big feet thwoking down, raising dust, demonstrating his sober control. As the dance went on he stamped as near to the offending spirits as a second skin would have been. His boots banged out a steady cadence. There was more spring in him than expected. The whole house rocked.

Mrs. Daily watched him. Her expression was nowhere near one of approval.

Finally Daily was flushed and satisfied and ended the jig with a tight, proud whirl. "Does that prove it? I never nudged it."

"You shame me," she said. "Only a drunk man would dance around that way."

This stunned him.

"Aw!" he went. He then lifted the jug and handed it to me.

I inspected the gift, then said, "It is uncracked, totally."

There was a pause and the woman used it to leave us again. But her purpose had been served. We passed the good cheer around one more circuit, then called it a night. We didn't want to sour a marriage by bad example.

Me and the boys rolled up on the floor but Daily would not go to bed. He hemmed and hawed fiercely for a while then went onto the front porch, with the jug, alone, and may well have drunk it all in his sulk.

It stymied me. I just didn't understand how it worked with a man and a woman. There was so much mystery involved. I hoped there could be a way around it.

In the morning every stream was high and the road was deep in cumbersome mud. We slopped through, all splattered and cranky. Our mood was foul and not unusual.

Gay birds perched about on wet, black branches, tweeting out their childish lullabies. Despite the muck, the day had a fresh feel to it. The sky was washed clean of clouds and the sun followed us like a smiley drummer peddling cures at half price.

But we were foul and not having any.

Poor Turner Rawls was swollen in the jaw, bloated up severely. He was alert but in constant pain. He would not complain, but as his horse clumsy-footed along he groaned pretty regular.

My finger root ached and ached still, but I had grown accustomed to it. In honest fact I was fond of the nubbiny wound, for I thought it might heal into something glamorous.

I felt a bond with these men. Where they would go so would I, where they fought I was dangerous and where they died I was sad.

I did not have it in me to ask for more. If my coffin is built longer than five feet and a half, the undertaker is posting me to Kingdom in my high-crowned slouch hat. For I am not large, but I have never felt too small to be of use. If I was handsome then, it was a secret, but I prided myself on looking *good enough* in tight spots.

★   ★   ★

McCorkle's farm came into view before morning had expired. Pickets challenged us and we answered correctly.

"Who are you?"

"Messengers of Good Work."

"Your banner?"

"The Black Flag."

In the camp we found a larger group of comrades. George Clyde had rendezvoused with us, doubling our numbers. Clyde was a stout, blocky man, with a strong Scot face. He was exceedingly popular, as he fought at the front when going that way, and the rear when backing up. His boys were good devout fighters and reckless.

Babe Hudspeth found his brother Ray and they hugged each other up. Ray had some slight scratch on him but it was a painless thing.

After our horses were staked out to graze, Jack Bull and I strolled the camp, checking the faces for those that were no longer there. Bill House was dead, killed in the run from the Rawlses' home, as was Pete Kinney, Dave Lane, Jim Martin and Cass Woods. Helms and Lawson were fried beneath the bed. The fight in the bush had claimed one more man, though not one I knew much. Two men were hurt bad enough to die but they likely wouldn't. They were tended to in the shade.

The guess was that we had killed six or eight Federals and wounded as many more. That sounded high to me. Our surprise had been so nearly complete that only divine good fortune had kept us from annihilation.

Cave Wyatt was whole, and clapped my back, generous with affection, a big grin on his broad bearded face.

"So glad you made it," he said. "I thought I would have no one left to pick on, but now you are here."

"Many aren't," I answered.

"True. But they died in the good fight. That is the best way to go."

I nodded, for this was the only sort of philosophy a freedom fighter could have if he was to avoid insanity.

"Let us hope we don't all go 'the best way,'" said Jack Bull. He was glumly staring about camp, no doubt brooding over the losses this war had already claimed from him. He would be wealthy no more, and, as he had been raised in that state, it was a bitter fate for him to accept.

It hurt me to see his manly face so forlorn, but I could not alter it.

As the day wore on I familiarized myself with Clyde's men. They had a surprise for us Ambrose Boys—four Federal prisoners. They had taken them from a mail convoy near Kansas City.

The Federals were tied more or less like yearlings, linked together by a thick rope, anchored to a tree. They trembled a bit and were skittish with their glances, not wanting to look too boldly into our faces.

Several of Clyde's group sat on the ground watching the prisoners, torturing them with bad jokes.

"Are those good boots, Yank?"

"I don't know. Could be."

"They seem to run a mite slow."

"This time they did."

"Well, there won't be any more races for them with you standing in them, will there?"

"I would reckon not."

"Ho, ho, ho. You are a shrewd reckoner, ain't you?"

One of the men who lounged there was the oddest comrade thinkable. It was George Clyde's pet nigger, Holt. He was always called Holt, and he carried pistols and wore our garb. It was said that he was an excellent scout and a useful spy. He looked about like any other nigger but spoke less and had a narrow quality to his face that gave it an aspect of intelligence.

Clyde's reputation served to protect Holt, but the nigger's actions also gradually gained him some esteem. He almost never spoke to anyone but Clyde, as he knew his opinions would be scorned. As with most niggers his life was puppeted by slender threads of tolerance at all times.

He was a good field cook, that was proven.

"Holt," I said to him as I stood.

His eyes came up to mine and held there steady, then he nodded once. There was a shiny effect from his gaze, as though some awful fire was in him. He did not speak.

"Jacob, oh, my Jacob," someone said to me. I slowly looked for the source and found it among the prisoners. There, hogtied to his poorly chosen comrades, was Alf Bowden, a neighbor of Jack Bull's and mine from near Waverly.

"Hello, Alf," I said. "You are in a fix."

"It seems so," he said. "It surely does seem so."

Gus Vaughn, an able bushwhacker, said to me, "You know this man?"

"Certainly," I said. I walked over and touched Alf on the shoulder. He seemed grateful for the display. His face was haunted by accurate expectations. "His little place was just downriver from the Chiles' place. Hemp grower."

Alf was sunken-chested and twig-thin. It was not uncommon to thus meet enemies who had not been so in gentler times. I had helped Bowden raise a barn once, and danced with his sister 'til her face flushed and we both sweated, but I was not in his debt, nor he in mine. It was a good war for settling debts via the Minié-ball payback or the flame of compensation. Many debts were settled before they had a chance to be incurred, but thin-skinned fairness rarely crabbed youthful aim.

I looked down at Alf. It seemed my presence was raising his hopes. Jack Bull Chiles then joined us, and Bowden strained his pale face, trying to summon up a grin.

"Jack Bull," he said.

Looking down his nose somewhat Jack Bull barely raised his chin in recognition. "Bowden," he said. "Any news of home?"

The little man started out shaking his head, but the gesture picked up momentum and soon his body shuddered entirely.

"No, no, no," he said. "It all goes on. It all just goes on. Some may have died, not most."

"What of our mothers?" Jack Bull asked.

"Well, now, well," said Bowden, his eyes angled down, "they are watched. All the secesh are watched."

"And my father?" I asked. I was vaguely interested in news of the old, exotic gent, but not frothy about it.

"He comes and he goes, like he always has. He ain't bothered by no one. No one hurts him. But, you know this, you must know the whole town knows you boys are out here, Black Flaggin' it." He finally glanced up. "Some friendliness may have been lost for your kin."

"Have you been fed?" Jack Bull asked.

"Not so's you'd notice."

"I'll look into it."

We left our old neighbor then, under the watchful eyes of Holt and the others. The camp was engaged in frolic. There was no rain on the wind, only the smell of thawed mud and early blossoms, but the boys were lazied by the previous days and made a carnival of the camp. A ball of leather was trotted out, and men of both groups began to boot it here and there. Their stomps turned the mud into a glue that sucked down boots and held them there.

"Will he be killed?" I asked Jack Bull.

"The odds are long in favor of it," he replied. "Unpleasant work, but necessary. Unless they can be traded. It seems Lloyd and Curtin got themselves took as prisoners at Lexington. A swap may well be in the works."

"Oh," I said. Usually we were shot on the spot, so the notion of a prisoner trade had not occurred to me. I looked back at the hog-tied Unionists, and sure enough, Alf Bowden watched me still. It would be sad to see him killed, but sadness was on the flourish in such times.

Each team of boys booting at the ball seemed determined

to win at the game. They flung themselves into blocks and shoved each other harshly. I suppose the tameness of such sport was comforting. But the whiskey had run low and this raised tempers. Little Riley Crawford, a mere boy, but one comfortable with grown-up moods, threw a kick of vigor that had no chance to contact the ball but plenty to shin Big Bob Flannery. And that is what happened. Flannery yowled, then cuffed Riley on the ears—you could see them redden smartly. Riley kicked him again, this time with no pretense of sport at all. After a yowl superior in emotion to the first, Flannery slammed a big, bony fist at the boy's head. He missed, though, and I saw steel in Riley's paw just as he slashed beneath Big Bob's armpit. A nice burst of blood patterned Flannery's shirt and he took a stagger backward.

Riley instantly knew he had done wrong. He began to walk away, hiding the knife.

"Oh, no," he said.

"I'm goin' to hurt you, boy!" Big Bob shouted. "You have forced me to it."

The youth turned back to him, his face a torture chamber of sensations—fear, shame and some pride showed.

"I'm sorry, Bob," Riley said. "It was a reflex. An instant thing. And you are *so* big."

"Hah!" went Flannery. "You ain't sorry yet!"

Big Bob headed toward the campsite, walking gingerly through the mud, holding his armpit, with Riley hopping after him at a safe distance. The boy was desperate to make it up to his comrade.

"I never meant it, Bob. I'll fix it for you. I'll fix it myself—

I know how. It's just a slash. Just a damn slash, your shirt took most of it. I *never* meant it to happen."

A number of the boys came forth to intercede. They reminded Flannery of past trials the two had shared, and the devotion they had shown one man to the other.

I watched the spectacle, curious about the outcome. It could be bad or beautiful. In a few minutes the peacemakers stood back. I could see the boy and the big man clearly. They stood next to each other, gazing like brothers into opposite eyes. Soon Big Bob pulled his border shirt up over his head, baring his white chest and thin red wound, and Riley spread a blanket on the ground.

Big Bob lay down, and it seemed to me that he enjoyed the attention. A sort of smile was on his face. The cut was not deep, more show than go, and Riley knelt down to wash it out with a bowl of water, his young fingers gently cleansing the forgiven slice.

It was an altogether inspiring scene to me. Proof that we shared something, that aloneness would not be our fate. We could forgive; it was a wonderful knowledge. And I was so glad for young Riley, for he had done wrong, but had been given a chance to allay his guilt immediately.

Would that more acts could be allayed that way. And, yes, would that more acts could be forgiven.

4

I HAD AN ODD talent: fine script. I was in much demand because of it. I often wrote letters for the men, and they claimed mine were an improvement on their own. It was a just claim.

Thus, when I was called to Black John's side and told to take down a note, it was a commonplace to me.

Black John sat drover-style, legs twisted beneath him, near a low fire. Pitt Mackeson and George Clyde were with him. Holt sat behind Clyde a small distance, ever watchful.

"Take this down," Black John said. His lips had spit dried on them and his eyes were tired and deep-looking. "It is for the *Lexington Union News,* so do it up fine the way you do."

"Gladly," I said.

"Dear Citizens," Black John orated. "Mistakes are most common these days and deadly for it. The Federals are to hang two fine sons of Missouri named William Lloyd and Jim Curtin. They are good men, too brave to accept any injustice. The rule of Federals is one such depravity they would not endure passively. Me neither.

"By a provident cut of the cards four Federals have been

dealt to me. They are Brown, Eustis, Bowden and Stengel. You know them. It is their hope that Lloyd and Curtin are not hanged, as they would provide the sequel to such murders.

"If Lloyd and Curtin are released I will, as a gentleman, release the above-named unfortunates. All are young men with much promise before them, or else a short dance from a stout tree.

"The choice is yours, citizens, make it wisely."

"Wait a minute," said Pitt Mackeson. "You need to tell the citizens we'll come and kill *them,* too."

"Oh, they *know* that," Black John said dryly. "It is understood." Black John chewed his lips for a moment, then added, "Signed, John Ambrose and George Clyde, Commanding, First Kansas Irregulars."

"That is good," said Clyde, who was at least an equal to Black John. "And put an extra note on it that says, 'Where you think we ain't, we are. Remember it!'"

I did so. It was a concise document, scripted in superior fashion. It would make a point well enough, I thought.

"Who will deliver it?" I asked. "There are Federals all over Lexington."

"We could slip a man in there," Mackeson suggested. "We have done it before."

"We have," said Clyde, "but it is always risky."

Black John hummed a snatch of a flat-note hymn, lolling his head this way and that in time to the tune, seemingly adrift from us. That was not the case, though.

"Oh, I reckon a citizen could be pressed into service," he said. "If one can be found."

"That might be a job," said I, "for citizens are cautious hereabouts."

"You got some better idea, Dutchy?" Mackeson asked. "Maybe you would volunteer yourself, eh?"

The notions were ill-defined but looming vaporous in the back half of my mind. Alf Bowden was all that I recognized in them, and I knew that I did not want to see him die. I scarcely was acquainted with the man, but even so slight a knowledge of him urged me to save him. This could be trouble, for some might see my merciful thinking as a traitorous bent.

"There is a way," I said, "to prove more things than one." I pointed toward the hog-tied Federals, and they were visible humps in the dim night, outlined against a flat expanse of soft-lighted countryside. "If we send a prisoner it will prove we have prisoners, and also he can attest to our intentions. It seems to me he could get more quickly to town, as well. And time is short. Curtin and Lloyd will be hanged right quick, I would think."

The hymn was rehummed by Black John, and all eyes present bunched up on me. It was rare that I made suggestions, for some slight suspicion of me worked against their acceptance.

Abruptly the lyricless hymn halted, and Black John said, "It is a good idea. There are some fine touches to it." He grasped my shoulder and gave me a squeeze. "You should speak up more, Roedel, for you are not near as dumb as you let on."

"Aw," I said.

Black John pushed up from the ground. Even his posture

was foreboding, as it was so stiff and straight. He was a man you could do nothing with but follow.

"Fetch some straw," he said. "We'll have the Federals do a drawing. Short straw travels."

This long-straw, short-straw method of pressing fate to make a decision was judged the fairest by boys and men. Many small choices had been made in this fashion: who will haul the water when ice is on the windows; who will ask the stout girl to dance so her comely friend will be available. But this decision was a larger one, yet the method employed was exactly the same.

Saving Alf Bowden was only slightly likely.

The Federals were brought into the light of a campfire. Their faces were so fraught with fears and hopes that it was uncharitable to watch them. They gave off an odor of close living and nervous secretions. It was a mess.

Arch Clay held the straws. It would not have been impossible for him to leave all the straws long, as sparing any Federal disgusted him. He leaned over the choosers, shading the straws with his free hand, a grin on his face.

"Pick your futures, boys," he said.

Bowden chose first. His hand trembled and he nearly drew two straws, but Arch clamped his fingers and only one slid out. It did not look especially short, either.

One of the prisoners, Stengel, was a foreigner pretty much. He was one of those worm-browed, dark Dutchmen with strong shoulders and bulbous cheeks. He pulled his straw coolly, and I knew the game was up, for it was winningly short and no mistaking it.

The game was completed with two more selections, but it was just exercise. Stengel would be the courier.

"Jacob," said Alf Bowden pitifully. "Jacob."

"This man," Black John said, resting a hand on top of Stengel's head, "will carry the letter to Lexington." He then patted the Dutchman's skull and said, "You are fortunate."

"*Ja,*" replied Stengel, peering into the ground between his knees.

Desperate Samaritanism consumed me. I nudged at Stengel with my boot. He looked up. My face felt twisted and hot atop my neck, and my lips, I knew, had flexed into a sneer.

" '*Ja! Ja!* ' " I said angrily. "This Dutch boater can't hardly talk American." I gestured at Black John. "How is he to present our case?"

Black John shrugged.

"As best he can," he replied.

"Lloyd and Curtin are lost if he is our courier." I looked about me to see how my theatrics were being received. " '*Ja, ja*' —hell, they'll not believe him for a minute."

"He is right," Pitt Mackeson said. For once his hatchet face looked on me fairly. "A goddamn lop-eared Dutchman — why it don't make sense to free him."

Black John slowly spoke. "Well, that is all well and good. But he won the draw."

Near me stood Jack Bull Chiles. His face had an empty expression, but his lips were ever so thinly curling up as if a grin hid in ambush behind them. I thought he nodded to me as though we had a secret. I could never conceal much from him.

"Straw pulling is just a game," I said. "Lives are at stake

here." I strode over to Alf Bowden, who was hunkered on the ground, and slapped his face. He grunted and turned away, so I leaned over and slapped him again. "Why, this man would present our case better than a lop-eared immigrant—you know it's so!"

Black John seemed to get taller. "You are not ready to be telling me what I know, Roedel. I will do that—always." His eyes burned into me and he did not speak for a nervous amount of time. "But I see your point. Send the American."

With that he turned and walked away, as did most of the men. Bowden began to whimper at my boots and I feared he might lick them.

"Get up," I said. I lifted his head by jerking a lock of hair. "Get up, you've got travel ahead of you."

Huge disappointment was at work on Stengel. He growled and tried to grapple with me, saying Dutch insults as he did so. I curled a crooked-armed punch that hooked him in the face. His nose went down and blood flooded his chin. This took the fight out of him but he still grumbled.

As Bowden was being cut totally loose of rope, I felt someone come stand behind me. I thought it was Jack Bull but, no, I faced about and it was Holt, the nigger.

"I am on to you, Roedel," he said softly, then walked backward, keeping his gaze fixed on me.

"Get too much on to me and I'll throw you off, Holt," I said. "A nigger is meaningless to me."

Even in the night I could see it—he actually smiled.

This was curious conversation with points that were uncertain, and disturbing. But then, what was not?

*   *   *

The letter was wrapped in oil paper and given to Alf Bowden. We put him astride a gimpy horse. Now that he was saved, his fright was lessened. He looked on me with less desperation and more anger.

"Do your best," I told him. "Show some sand or these men will die because you didn't."

He did not reply, but set off in the deep dark, picking his way toward Lexington. There had been no sign of thanks in him at all.

Gratitude is such an infant's expectation, always, but it is one I only slowly outgrew. He might have said something.

Salt pork and oatcakes fueled the next day. The boys sat in comfortable clusters, oiling pistols and limbering jawbones. George Clyde, who had been born in Dundee, Scotland, acted as a Plato or Socrates might have, staggering us with questions.

"If a six-teated dog runs ten miles an hour shittin' splinters, how swift need she be to shit a rockin' chair?"

The answers were various, speculative and joyous. A scientific facet was revealed in Gus Vaughn, who said the dog must probably be swimming to shit a rocking chair whole, though she might drop it in pieces while napping after eating a possum belly.

"Boys," Clyde said when the first query had been exhausted. "What I most want to know in the world is this: who thought up bagpipes anyhow? It is a grave issue if you've ever heard one played."

The day went by with these stumpers, and it was as good a way as any to pass the time. There was turmoil in us. If Lloyd and Curtin were murdered, we would have bitter tasks ahead of us, and soon. Silliness provided a sweet and momentary refuge.

In that one day the Federals made up for all the bedtime prayers they had ever skipped. There was a ceaseless babble of holy hopes and galloping confessions coming from them.

We could not tolerate Federals, for they oppressed us in our fight for freedom. Many of them were not Missouri men, or even Kansans, but killer dupes from up the country two or more states away. Their presence freed maniac Jayhawkers to ravage about the countryside, taking all of value back to Kansas with them.

Jayhawkers said they raided to free slaves, but mostly they freed horseflesh from riders, furniture from houses, cattle from pastures, precious jewelry from family troves and wives from husbands. Sometimes they had so much plunder niggers were needed to haul it, so they took a few along. This, they said, made them abolitionists.

They were dangerous sneak-murderers, the Jayhawkers were. They had killed hundreds of us one or two by the time, but never faced us in open battle. They kept to the woods and followed the Federals, striking hard when the odds were trivial.

In this they were much like us—but terrible.

The hours of the night taunted me by passing slowly, ever so slowly, and dull. Sleep outran me and I had little to do but squat beneath green-leaved branches and paw over things in my head. Killing and war were nothing I had expected in life. Before shots became the answers to the grand debate, I was common and fortunate. Asa Chiles, a good American, had been fond of me and Jack Bull, my near brother. Citizens had not darkly speculated against my character.

Now they did. Woof and warp had hit the border. Blood had been let, a reasonable share of it by me. The Dutch boy was a tragedy of necessity lest I be the actor in a more severe scene. Some would hold this against me. My good reputation had no doubt been splattered lately as certain of my deeds became known. But I was not so paltry a specimen that a bit of sullying would defeat me. If all meals were pecan pie, you'd yearn for a cold potato.

Jack Bull, my comfort and cause, roused from his blanket beside me. As I looked at his fine American face, I hoped it would always be this way—him and me and little else.

"You are brooding," he said. "Dutchmen brood too much. Break yourself of that."

"You brood, too, Jack Bull."

He sat up with his legs before him, elbows atop his knees. His slouch hat was shoved back on his crown. Long curls of hair nuzzled at his neck.

"I have some things to brood about, Jake."

"And I don't?"

"In your way I suppose you do. What I have lost you have sort of lost, as you would have always shared in it. You know that."

"True," I said. "And your father was nearly mine."

"No," Jack Bull said with a layer of scrape in his tone. "No. He was a kind and good man to you, but, no. He was my *blood*. Anything less than that is *less* than that."

His despair diverted me from my own and I wanted to put some happy back into his smart face. I wanted to say something about good coming from bad and so on, but it is a form of Sunday School lunacy to suggest that such could be the case in the murder of your father, and the destruction of your home.

"We'll stick together," I said. "And get all of it back."

"Hah! You are a black magician who can raise the dead, are you? No you are not! No one is. Daddy is under the dirt to stay." Jack Bull's head was flung about on his neck and he growled. It was an exercise to shake off foul memories. "And that," he said, pointing at my nubbined left hand, "is gone to stay gone, too."

"So it is," I replied. "And it makes me notable by the loss."

"You sound pleased, as if that finger had been pestering you for rings."

"Well, no. It was a fine finger—I'll not deny it." I held the nubbin up and wiggled the stump. "See that? Can you see that? I'm the only man you know who can do that."

Jack Bull was a rock for some seconds, his eyes stony on me. Then his dandy head nodded.

"That is true," he said, his head gyrations slowly changing from nods to shakes. "And I don't know any noseless men who spit tobacco juice so it squirts from between their eyes either, Jake. A no-nose tobacco squirter could name his price on the stage, I would reckon."

"Oh, there is mud everywhere you look anymore, Jack Bull." I wiggled my nubbin some more and said, "I'd rather *have* my finger, but it was took from me. It has been et by chickens for sure. So, I say to myself, 'What is the good side to this amputation?' And there is one."

"Name it. I'll just have to ask you to name it, Jake."

"I intend to. Say, now just say, if I was on the move with you and Riley and Cave. Say that. And two hundred Federals came onto us and my horse was shot. Dead."

"I'd pull you up behind me, Jake."

"I know it," I said. "But, now, say your horse was shot and floundered down, and Cave was gone and Riley pulled *you* up behind *him*. And I was left. Say that."

"Hey," Jack Bull whispered. "I might *unload* Riley and save you. Those things happen."

"Oh, God damn it, Jack Bull! That ain't where I'm going. Will you listen to me? I'm trying to explain the good that comes from bad for you." I stirred the dirt beneath me, collecting my thoughts, then rejoined my previous tale. "And you escaped, okay? Well, I would take to the bush, wouldn't I? And I would punch leaks in ten Federals before they killed me in such a thicket. But eventually they would riddle me and hang me from a way tall limb like they do. No southern man would find me for weeks or months, and when they did I'd be bad meat. Pretty well rotted to a glob."

"That is scientifically accurate," Jack Bull said. "I'm afraid I've seen it."

"I would be a glob of mysterious rot hanging in a way tall tree, and people would ask, 'Who was that?' Surely, sometime somebody would look up there at my bones and see the telltale stump and reply, 'It is nubbin-fingered Jake Roedel!' Then you could go and tell my mother I was clearly murdered and she wouldn't be tortured by uncertain wonders. Now do you see the tenderness of it all? It's there if you look."

The night air was chilled for pleasant breathing, and trees rustled just enough to soothe. Pickets were out in the moonlight and the faint snores of comrades droned nearby. I felt I was where I should be; I had bushwhacked my way into these slumbering hearts.

"I care for you," Jack Bull said to me. He then lay down and rolled up in his blanket. His hat covered his face but he spoke through it. "I do care for you, but, Jake, it is sometimes a very nervous thing."

5

Black John Ambrose had a tough-thunk vision and there were no quibbles left in it. When the word arrived he went straight toward Stengel, the Federal who'd once had two minutes of good luck.

The centerpiece of Stengel's face was colored ocean blue and lumpy from when I'd chastised him. He looked bad enough but quickly got worse.

"Dead, dead," declared Black John. "Hanged like dogs would be if dogs were less respected. Yes, oh my, yes. They have went and done it to us."

Black John used his pistol as a club and batted Stengel in the face, cracking him open above the brow. An animal-panic chorus of grunts came from the prisoners, even those yet to be damaged, as they sized up the future to be one of pain.

We all stood silent in the morning light, encircling the Federals. Many faces were sad, even squeamish, about the necessaries of the day. But several faces were poised with a hunger for the hot plate of revenge they'd been served. Lloyd and Curtin had been hung, then quartered and tossed onto the River Road to nourish varmints. The quartering was meant to disturb us, and in at least one case, it worked.

"They hung our comrades," Black John said. "And ripped them to fragments." He slapped iron on Stengel's face and Stengel hunched over so as to take the raps on the head. Black John looked down on the Federal, then opened both hands and began to squeeze Stengel's head. His feely search had him all about the Federal noggin for some seconds, caressing and patting, then he stepped back. His face exhibited the pleasure of discovery. "Your skull," he said somberly, "will make a European palace for our worms, eh?"

"Uh, uh, uh," went Stengel.

One of the other Federals began to puff in the jowls and burp. He did it rapid-fire and Black John turned to him.

"Don't you agree, Yank?" Black John inquired. He then did the melon test on Stengel's head again. "A palace for worms, eh?"

Burping frights racked the Federal but finally he mastered them enough to speak.

"Yes, sir, yes, sir, yes, sir, yes, sir..."

Black John reared back and kissed Stengel hard in the face with his pistol. The nose went different ways, and Dutchy spluttered for breath through a tide of blood.

The other Federal saw this and changed his litany.

"Oh, no, oh, no, oh, no..."

The scene was not good. A pink spray of misery spittled on the wind. The prisoners were doomed but trifled with. All common sense dictated that they must die, but better deaths could be arranged in my mind. It was all too near to what I expected for myself.

"Here is what your people said," George Clyde called out. He unfolded a wad of newspaper and held it flat to read from.

" 'War is loss, but capitulation is devastation. Good men will die until all bad ones have. William Lloyd and James Curtin were proven to be worse than bad can cover. They have perished. Their deaths illustrate our resolve. I have no doubt that the disloyal terrorists have already murdered our soldiers. I have much experience of these vermin. To negotiate would have been foolish. Therefore it was not done. Thomas B. Hovland, Commanding First Iowa.' " Clyde rattled the paper ceremoniously, then folded it back into a pocket square. "You should have better chosen your comrades, boys. To save our own, *we* would do anything."

Black John raised himself to a stern posture and spit twice. He then said, "Have at them, boys, and make it memorable. We want them to be mementos of *our* resolve."

Pitt Mackeson and Turner Rawls, whose jaw was still several colors and swollen, joined Arch Clay in administering slow disaster to the prisoners. I did not want to watch, but I did not want to be seen turning away. Howard Sayles, Josiah Perry and several other men did leave the festivities, but they made no comment as they lumbered away.

I was saved by Black John calling to me.

"Roedel, come here to me."

He stood on a small rise of earth overseeing the action, pacing this way and that, a white froth scabbing at the corners of his mouth. "Take down this note!"

"Certainly, Black John. Let me fetch my implements." I very quickly did so, then squatted on the dirt near his feet. "I am ready."

"Good, good," he said. His eyes were of a pale gray hue

and had no bottom to them. "I have three sisters, Roedel. Have you any? They are as good as you could expect them to be. I kill for them. They are women and can't fight. I can. The world knows I can. And I do. I do fight. Hard. I am awful but right. Never doubt it." He nudged my knee with the pointed toe of a boot. "Do you doubt it?"

"No. No, I never doubt it. I believe."

"Do you believe in me, or our cause?"

"I believe in me and you and our cause."

"Be leery of where you place your faith," Black John said. The oaths and laments, the cracks and smacks, the prayers and punishments went on below the small rise. We both looked there. "This is a time of infinitely shaded cruelty, Roedel. It cannot be otherwise. I have victory in mind." Suddenly he whirled and leaned over me. His countenance had a wrathful cast, and spit flew from his lips like a nasty rain. "*Take this down!* 'Citizens, you have stood by for murder. Another of your mistakes, which you have made plenty of. This ruin is yours to claim. Look at them and recall it. Remember this, townspeople: you will not escape me for long. You may fool me for a minute or an hour or a day. But you will not forestall me long enough that I forget the path to your town. No, I will remember it, and at some good moment pull you from your beds and use an inch rope to put all you oppressors face-to-face with more truth than you can tolerate.

"'You have placed your bets, now wait for the next turn of cards.'"

The paper trembled in my hand and my hand wobbled my

arm to the shoulder. I could not look up and I longed for a brief spell of deafness.

"What shall I do with this note?" I asked.

"Pin it to the breast of one of the unfortunates, in clear sight." Black John was calmed in a coiled sort of way. "We will dump them on the road tonight. It will get read, I am certain of that."

Black John stared once more at the killing going on, his face flat with resolute anger. Then he stalked off without a word to me or a shout or a glob of spit coming from him.

The knot of men, crouched, half bent or standing, who encircled the unfortunates, parted for me. There were many heavy breaths being drawn, and Pitt Mackeson sucked on a sore knuckle.

"I have a letter," I said. "A note. Black John wants it pinned on one of them."

I looked down at the Federals. A violent rapture had caught up with them. I had seen harsh errands performed before, but not like this. Some dark appetites had been brought forth in this spectacle, and my comrades had revealed themselves to be near wizards at unpleasantries.

And yet one of the Federals breathed. It was an exercise he was about beyond performing, and he strained in the effort.

I was all confused up in my sensations. I just stood there.

Arch was knelt down going through pockets. He had a handful of letters he'd taken from the doomed. He jerked open the shirt of the live one and recovered a letter hidden there, then thumped his fist on the bare chest.

"Pin it on him," he said. "We'll set *him* up pretty. He lived longest."

When I put my knees to ground and leaned over the Federal, he lurched up and I reared back.

"My wife," he whispered. "Write my wife."

Arch laughed and held in front of me the letter he had ransacked.

"This must be from her. I can't read to tell."

I pinned Black John's sermon to the Federal's tunic. He was flat again but breathing.

When I stood Arch said, "Read me this letter, Dutchy."

"That's *his* letter," I said.

"Was," said Arch. "I want to hear you read it."

"I don't think I care to."

"Oh, is that so?" drawled Arch. His eyes sank behind his lids and his mouth hung open. "I think if you think a little more, Dutchy, that you'll think you *do* want to read me it. Right now, too."

"Yes," said Pitt Mackeson. "Why, there might be secrets in it. Read it at us."

I scented trouble with my comrades if I showed a dainty spirit here. The prospect was not delicious.

The script on the letter had bold girlish leaps and bounds to it, with circles above the *I*'s. It was addressed to Corporal Miller Eustis.

I began to read the letter aloud, and acted as if I enjoyed the process. The first many lines were without secrets, and mainly contained a young wife's version of everyday events in Mount Vernon, Iowa. It seemed the Methodists wanted a school there to prosper, and the Cedar River had flooded, and old Ben Eustis had snapped a big toe kicking at a growling dog.

A new mood was then hove into the letter, and the wife said she loved this pink thing on the dirt before me with a devotion that would not wane.

The boys chuckled at this, as though the love of a Yankee woman had no merit. But I was envious in a way. There was a straight-ahead womanness to this author, and I found it admirable.

Eustis, the Federal, had lost where he was and spoke to people who were not nearby. He said friendly things to them. It was good that his soul had started aloft, for there was a secret in this letter that made me ashamed.

"'Miller, Miller,'" I read, "'I miss you so. I miss your cool brow and warm brown eyes. The way your cheeks crease when you smile. It makes me crazy, but I most miss your tender red-faced turtle head atop that sweet length of neck. I dream of petting him so special that he drools into my palm and I lick my fingers for a taste of you.'"

The boys about shattered themselves with rude laughter upon hearing this.

"My Lord," said Arch, all manner of unpleasant glee reflected in his face. "Them Yank gals! Them *Yank* gals! Why, only a whore would say that."

The Federal now thrashed about some. He may have understood. It was pitiful.

"No southern woman would say such a thing," Pitt Mackeson said. "Ho, ho! I *cain't wait* to be in charge of *Iowa!*"

I couldn't stand it. The Federal gurgled and the boys said, "Tender turtle head! Tender turtle head!" real loud.

So I shot him where he lay and put a period to the letter. My act was sudden and it stalled the boys' laughter.

I walked off with my Colt cocked and my step steady.

Not a word was said to me.

Later on I lounged about, trying to dredge up the tart taste of a jenniton apple in my memory, and the perfumed-sweat smell of real ladies waltzing all night with someone else at a levee dance, and the gushing warmth I'd always felt when Asa Chiles had tousled my hair and called me lucky.

But all that past was a sluggish slough, and I could not flow it up to me at all.

My thoughts were just of now or tomorrow.

Jack Bull Chiles was near me but did not speak for a great stretch of time. He had been a bystander to the day but never an active part of it.

"Say, Jake," he eventually said, "what are you knowing?"

"I feel I am knowing too much."

"Ah. Well, forget it. Throw it down."

"Once you are knowing it, that is hard to do."

"Oh, hell, Jake. Too much knowledge is only a form of torture. You can do nothing with it but recognize a wider variety of agonies."

As a philosopher my near brother was aimed in always on the practical. If a notion will pass the night for you, and lead you into another day, then believe it.

"Dogs fight," I said. "We fight, as well. It could be we settle too many squabbles by the dog method."

"Hah," Jack Bull said. "Hah, young Roedel, you are sounding like some terrifically moustached old kraut grov-eler at this moment." He slapped a hand on my boot. "And that is not you. That is not you. You are an American."

I felt like this meant I had the farm but not the crop.

There would be more harsh errands to be done, this I knew, and I would do them. I knew that as well. I was in this fight to fight.

"We could have merely shot them," I said. "No gain would have been missed if we had merely shot them instead of whipping them raw."

Jack Bull called up a glob of crud and spit it out. He rubbed his nose and looked away, then shrugged and looked back.

"That was not the plan," he said. "There may seem to be no rhyme to it, but that was just plain old *not* the plan."

What else could I say but, "You are right."

6

THAT NIGHT A certain sort of apology, or so I chose to view it, was tendered me as a result of my earlier oration. Arch and Pitt and Turner ambled over to me and dropped at my feet all the letters they had plundered.

"You might read 'em," Arch said. "I won't."

"Can't," said Pitt.

"Won't 'cause I can't," Arch admitted.

"Take these with 'em," Pitt said. He dropped a cloth satchel of mail they'd found when they first took the prisoners. "There's not a thing of use in here, Black John says. Just home letters and relative talk."

This gift was an outlandish gesture for my comrades to make.

"Why?" I asked. "Why give the letters to me?"

"Oh," Arch said, and stammered around on his feet a bit. "Oh, we just figured you might find a thing or two of use in them. That's all. That's what we figured."

"I don't know what it would be," I said.

"Aw, hell!" Pitt snapped. "Read 'em or burn 'em, Dutchy! Whatever you want to do, you do it!"

Turner sat beside me then, and Arch and Pitt walked away. They seemed to think I had not been gracious.

Rustling his hand in the pouch, Turner found a letter that he pulled out. He held it toward me.

"Woot dat tay, Yake?"

His mouth parts were still out of step, and he was a good man, but mocking him was not a safe idea.

I held up the piece of mail.

"It says, 'For delivery to John Plater or Dave Plater, Fourth Wisconsin Cavalry, Liberty, Missouri.'" I looked at poor swollen Turner. He was trying to be a comrade to me. "It's from Wonowoc, Wisconsin, Turner. Ever been that far north?"

"Uh-uh." He shook his head and his long hair flopped about. "Neber no weason to go dat fur nort."

"Nor I," I said.

"Weed it," Turner mumble-mouthed. He hunkered toward me, grinning like a boy. "Cood oo weed id ad me?"

There was the thick odor of woodsmoke wafting from clothes and persons. We had been in the bush a good long while and our scent proved it. Perhaps a piece of mail would bolster spirits, but we never had any that was meant for us. We were not alone but lonely, and a trifle queasy about who we were.

"Yes, Turner. I'll read it at you." I popped the wax seal back with my thumb and unfolded the paper. The script was black and spidery and spotted. An unfirm hand had beared down on this note. "'Dear sons,'" I read. "'No word of you in so long. Right past first frost of the year last. Father worries. His feet are bloated and he won't walk right on them.'"

At this point Babe and Ray Hudspeth, Jack Bull, Josiah Perry, Holt the nigger, Riley Crawford and Big Bob Flannery wandered to hear me read. They all squatted in a clump and looked on me raptly.

"That's thicked-up blood does that," Josiah said. He had just a patch of face showing between his beard and hair, and his body was ox-size. "Thicked-up blood bloats the feet."

"Uh-huh," I said, then read on. " 'A fire hit the old church. Burned down. The new one was just ready so no great trouble was had of it. No pigs was lost. Margaret has married since the frost of this year last. You wouldn't know it for how could you. Her husband is Walter Maddox. He is out of the war. One arm was busted up at New Madrid but it works fine enough. This spring the dirt was turned over and the smell and deepness gave me heart. It is just black-rich and feels good in the hand. You boys know how that is.' "

"My daddy was up there," Riley said. His thin young face was bright with recollection. "He was up there once long ago, long ago, way before they hung him. He said the dirt was so rich you could eat it like porridge."

"They have very good dirt up there," Jack Bull said. "But a short grow season."

"It sounds like *real* good dirt to me," Riley said. "Daddy told me it was."

I read on.

" 'Louetta Hines tells me Bernard Lafton from over at Suskanna Creek is dead in the war. Bless his soul. He was at Tennessee and tick fever got him. That girl Dave got sweet for is in town and still single and about. She asks of you but I have no news since first frost of the year last. Without news I cannot answer her.'"

The boys were somber listening to this. For so many of us, home was now the place where we were most likely to be recognized and killed. This was not always the case, and even where it was the odds were often bucked for a good strong mother hug.

"'I hope and father hopes you will write more. Do you need anything just ask. The seed is in the ground now tho you both are missed there is that to give thanks for. Little green sprouts will soon poke up and look good. Your Mother.'"

The men were lulled silent for a moment, then Riley, the youngest of us all, said, "She sounds about like my mother, that old woman does."

"One mother is much like another," Jack Bull said. "But don't be fooled by a mother's words, Riley. Her boys will kill you if they can. Remember that."

"I pretty much always do, Jack Bull."

I folded the letter back up, then tapped the square of it on my knee and my leg bounced a sit-down jig, mashing my boots in the dirt.

"You know, boys," I said, and I was looking to the tree-tops while my heels jumped on the earth, and all these hard boys and the nigger stared on me, and I held the letter up and waved it like a battle flag. "Boys, this is a *wonderful* big country."

BOOK TWO

Equality of reward is out of the question.

— PIERCE EGAN

7

I WAS BORN ON a cold dark wave, pitched high to be dropped low, somewhere between Hamburg and Baltimore. The tale was often told to me. I squalled belowdecks and bounced on the ocean, a hungry new thing sprung on the world, far at sea.

Missouri was the promised land for Germans. Newspapers in the Old World printed glowing accounts of it and a rush of immigrants headed for the cheap land, thick-wooded rolling hills and good water of the state. My father was a vintner and my mother a vintner's wife. It was that simple.

My first memory is of steamboats hooting by on the Big Muddy. Picnics were made of their passing, Americans and immigrants alike gathering on river bluffs to watch them churn upriver or down.

As that springtime of war baked into a hot dangerous summer, these thoughts came often to me. The days were filled with strife and hurting and long rides. We galloped up on Federal convoys at Blue Cut and Quick City. In both instances they fought back a little. It was brave of them. None was spared.

By night my thoughts roamed when possible.

Asa Chiles often came to mind. Jack Bull's father was a tall man, with hair the shade of iron, and a firm chin. His mouth was small and tight, but it could stretch into a smile that was wide enough. My father worked for him in the vineyards, as Asa Chiles's *Winzer,* for Asa had a dream of great wines being made in Missouri. The plantation was mainly concerned with hemp growing, but a good chunk of it was set aside for grape experiments.

In late July Josiah Perry went to visit his family in Cass County. We received word that he was killed soon thereafter, murdered by a Unionist named Arthur Baines who lived in that area. It made us all sad, and angry, so we went to the funeral, seventy-five riders strong by now, for new men were driven to us in the bush every day.

A few of the townspeople were glad to see us and the Perry family seemed proud of the high regard we showed for Josiah. We were shot in the neck with much good whiskey, but even that did not make me fond of the town. There was a pinched look to the whole of it, and pinched well and good it had been. That whole half of Missouri was being pinched and put to waste by Jayhawkers, Federals and militia. There were so many of them that we could be but a wrong nail in their boots, painful to walk on but not crippling.

We did what we could for our people.

After a sweet-sung funeral we found Arthur Baines at his home. The nearby presence of Federals gave him too much confidence. We pulled him into the yard as his family wailed.

"Josiah Perry was a traitor and a thief," Baines cried. He had some sand in him. "You are all traitors and thieves, too!"

A ball took effect in his chest, then, and he insulted us no more.

That was one harmful scene I was glad to be a part of. Josiah Perry, bless his clean white soul, had been a fine comrade, and retribution is necessary to keep any balance.

In the years gone by Jack Bull had had a brother named Stoddard, but he drank a cup of bad milk and died at one. It was a tragedy to the family, and no new brother could be borne by Missus Chiles.

My father had a cabin not two hundred yards from the main house. There was no more than one season in age between Jack Bull and me. Missus Chiles came of the Bulls from Frankfort, Kentucky, and had a delicate spirit. After the burial of Stoddard she brooded for weeks, then began to stroll down the dirt rut to our cabin in the afternoons. My parents spoke almost no English, which was still more English than they wanted to speak, but Missus Chiles made her wishes plain. Me. She wanted to bounce me around, on her knees, on the dirt and high in the air, demonstrating a wide range of robust affection, then soothe me with gurgles and sweets. It was a routine that won me over, and her as well. Soon I was at the main house, with its spread of rooms, wide veranda, and house niggers fluttering about, from dawn to dusk.

As is the general rule with babes, Jack Bull and me found no fault with each other, but discovered a vast world full of slobbering adventures that we took best together.

My parents were treated well, and, at night, when I was once more in their orbit, stared on me in a stupefied way. I spoke English like a jackdaw by age six, and this skill annoyed them. I had had a baby brother named Luther and a sister called Heidi, but neither of them lived a week and I recalled them only as graves. My father, Otto, was kind and my mother kinder.

But Asa Chiles was fascinating. As far as you could see, he owned. No one dared pass him in the street without a greeting. His wing shot was hell on edible birds, and he rode horses in a manner that would put a Comanche's nose out of joint. There was no one day that made him my idol, but a long succession of days in which he was hero to them all.

My father grew vines, and grumbled about this and that, most often in the company of other cranky Dutchmen who wore moustaches down to their necks and found very little to their liking. They had come to Missouri for a fresh start, but wasted their free time by attempting to model this new land on the old land they had been so eager to flee. The great sense in this never struck me.

I was as American as anybody.

Our mode of warfare was an irregular one. We were as likely to be guided by an aged farmer's breathless recounting of a definite rumor, or by the moods of our horses, as we were by logic. It was a situation where logic made no sense. So we slouched about in wooded areas, our eyes on main roads and cow paths, watching for our foe to pass in reasonable numbers.

They often did.

The windy flab-grunts of the dying were a regular sound in our days. When the fray was joined, and blood raced to my extremities, things occurred to me and I did them. At Rush Bottom I blasted down two wagoneers who made a feeble attempt on my life with a shotgun. I noted that their faces flooded with expressions of sweet fantasy just as I worked my trigger. Some pleasant falsehood had been their last thought.

As we slithered over hills and down valleys and through great forests, we acted out sudden tragedies for many a luckless oppressor. No amount of troops could protect them all, and we drove that point home.

We were whimsical about destruction. Bridges, barns, homes—now you have it, now no one does. Flames all a-crackle and us in swift retreat was a common scene.

I had not the education to understand all of this. I could read, yes, and write. Some ciphers were known to me and Asa Chiles's library had sailed me to places I would never see. Asa was a huge admirer of Homer, and George Borrow, William Cobbett, Pierce Egan the Elder, Shakespeare and Sir Walter Scott. The Bible had been mauled by my hands also. But this was nowhere near enough.

Late in August we were on the Blackwater, riding past a sloppy fence that surrounded the ashes of a home and a standing chimney. On the fence posts were the heads of two of our occasional comrades. They were ripe and pecked. Black John said we must bury them. We searched and searched but could not find them below the neck.

A year earlier this would have sickened me beyond

consolation for days. But we were hardened youths by that point. Warfare was what we knew. Though we were mostly still boys by civil calculations, we had by now roughed up the swami and slept where the elephant shits. Shocking us would have required some genius.

I remembered this: Missus Chiles pulling me by the ears, then cupping my chin in her hands and saying, "I like having you in the house, Jacob, my boy. I just enjoy the noise of it so much."

Such recollections were nourishing to me. I was a good child and hoped I had become the man you would have predicted from my tyke version. It is hard to know.

Guns had always figured in my life. When Jack Bull was given an overweight, aimless shotgun at age eight, one was soon found for me. We kicked through brier patches and shocked rabbits with our thunder, but it took time before we could hit any. That didn't matter. Even as we missed our targets, we imagined ourselves to be kids who would grow into dangerous men, perhaps the sort who had whipped Mexico or England.

Asa took us in hand and taught us things. We learned to bow to ladies and touch two fingers to our hat brims on passing men. "Manners won't cost you a thing," Asa said. "But they may gain you plenty."

When the first chill winds blew in our faces, we became furious in our need to put on some hurts before full winter arrived. The tempo of our deeds increased to a crescendo.

At Latour we were fired on, Cave Wyatt being wounded. Three citizens paid for it and Arch did some bad-dream alterations on heads and bodies, striving for more comical fits. We burned houses and stole clothes, silver and garish trash, sometimes overloading our mounts, so acquisitive had we become.

When the leaves were giving it up and falling, Gus Vaughn returned from a trip. He sat with Jack Bull and me, his big red face looking somber.

"I have news of home," he said. "Hank Pattison is murdered. Our old neighbor, Jantzen, got him with his gang of militia."

"That is sad," Jack Bull said. "He was a good southern man and friend. What of Thomas Pattison?"

"Oh," Gus said, "he is murdered, too. Jantzen was on a bloody spree thereabouts."

"That Jantzen was a bad man before he was a man," Jack Bull said fiercely. "Where has he gone with his militia?"

"He goes nowhere now. The son of a bitch got what was coming to him. Thrailkill's boys looked him up and he got what was by God coming to him."

"I wish it had been us," I said.

"Sally Burgess married a Federal from Michigan," Gus said. "Her whole family hides their faces."

"Any other news?" I asked.

"Well, yes, Dutchy. Alf Bowden killed your father." Gus pulled his hat off and held it in his hands. "Bowden shot him in the neck down by the river, then booted him along Main Street 'til he died."

Jack Bull's hand went to my shoulder and my heart pumped bad blood-thoughts to my head.

"My father," I said. "My father was an Unconditional Unionist. Like all the Germans. An Unconditional Unionist."

"Well, yeah," Gus said. "But he was mainly known as your father, Dutchy. You got a reputation."

"I spared Bowden," I said. My mind was in a whirl, and a mix of unpleasant ideas came to me. "You know it. I know you know it. I spared Bowden."

"It didn't make a friend of him," Jack Bull said. "You taught him mercy but he forgot the lesson."

"Both your mothers went to Kentucky," Gus went on. "By train, I think."

I felt my face warp and wobble and my arms quaked. I could have cried. Gray heads suffered while young ones went unnoosed.

"I might as well have shot him myself," I said. "Mercy has treachery in it. I need to forget I know of it. I'll put it aside. I am not too brilliant with it."

"That may be the answer," Jack Bull said.

Oh, everything happens.

8

WHEN ALL THE trees were bare, we had trouble. We suffered fearful subtractions. John Colbert was killed. Lafe Pruitt, Ralph Sawyer, Randolph Haines and Joe Loubet were cut off in a range of trees and hunted down, then blasted neutral by a large squad of Federals. Wounds were as likely as sunup. It was a miserable season to fight in.

Where it was possible we balanced things. At Holden we found a handful of militia, and Riley, Jack Bull and me did all the balancing. Five graves would be filled whenever someone took the trouble to dig them. We looted the Holden store and found forty pair of boots. The boots smelled finely of fresh leather, and in a corner of the store there was also a whiskey barrel. We punched holes in the boot tops, strung them together with rope, then bashed in the barrel and filled them with Old Crow. We hung the whiskey-sloshing boots about our necks like nooses, and drank by kicking up the heels.

Just into December Black John and George Clyde decided we must disband until spring. Our large group was too easily located by larger groups of the enemy when we were so slowed by the season. Our plan was to go off and hide in groups of four, surviving the winter as best we could.

Our breaths gave off clouds that wafted in the air and we stamped the ground to warm our feet. There were nervous looks in many faces. Small groups might be more easily hidden but if found it would be awful hot.

As the cold wind slapped red on our cheeks and our nervous eyes went here and there, Black John Ambrose put on a 'til-we-meet-again-in-the-spring speech. When Black John's ideas were spelled out plain, it was sometimes less good than confusion had been. He shouted about the cloven foot of tyranny and the Founders of our Nation and bodiless comrades and blue-bellied murderers who were even now sniffing close to our women and how wonderful the feel of an oppressor's blood is when it dries on your hands. It went on and on.

When his speech was played out the boys raised a couple of huzzahs and hoorahs. He accepted the acclaim with the coolness of an uncaught caesar.

Then we all parted, heading for secret caves, or far-in-the-woods relatives, or friendly southern strangers, to wait out the bad weather.

Jack Bull, me, George Clyde, Riley, Turner, the Hudspeths and Holt went the first leg of our journey together. At Captain Perdee's farm we split up. Jack Bull and me and Clyde and Holt went on to the neighborhood of a certain miss named Juanita Willard. Clyde was sweet on her, but we could not stay safely on the Willard farm. This fact brought us to the nearby place of Jackson Evans.

Jackson Evans had been a friend to Asa Chiles. At one

time the Evans place had been highly prosperous and he'd owned more niggers than anyone in those parts.

Things had changed.

The Evans household held Jackson, his wife, a small girl called Honeybee but whose right name was Mary, and a teenaged girl who was the widow of Jackson's son, Jackson, Junior. Junior had been killed at Independence in the house-to-house fighting after only a few weeks of marriage. The widow girl was named Sue Lee and her maiden name had been Shelley.

All the niggers were gone to Kansas or into the Federal Army. The farm had a very lonely feel to it, for it was plain that it had been designed for dozens to live there. And they had once—but no more.

A layer of hills were closed in around the farm like some feminine embrace. George Clyde and Jack Bull selected a likely spot among the humps and we started to dig in. To stay in the house would be ridiculous. Patrols passed by plenty.

Jackson Evans loaned us shovels and a pickax and we went to it, slamming away through the thin frozen topsoil. Holt and I switched off on the pickax while George and Jack Bull did the shoveling.

The day was gray, though not moist. It was cool, but a good clean sweat came up from the work.

"It has been a while since we've done work," Jack Bull said. "There is something soothing about it."

George Clyde laughed, his wide, square face splitting. He was not hard to like but terrible to cross.

"Work has never been my main ambition," he said. He

laughed more and patted Holt on the shoulder. "We have done much work—just look at these hands—but I think I've spied an easier way to riches."

"Spell out this miracle," Jack Bull said.

"Why," Clyde said, "you just ride up with the boys and *take* it."

"Ah, it's the good old rule, the simple plan," Jack Bull sang. "Those who would should take, and those should keep who can."

"Exactly," said Clyde. "It's a workable method—that is proven."

George Clyde and Jack Bull Chiles shared the nature that adapts quickly to the practical, but it was still inconvenient to my mind. It was the difference between What? and Why? Though I might rob, I did not believe myself as a robber.

"I don't know that the time is yet right for robbing wholesale," I said.

Clyde scooped a shovelful of dirt, then flung it aside. He grinned at me.

"You don't know enough, then," he said. "I think it is as right as two rabbits."

I looked at his face and decided that I would differ with him on this but not make a debate of it.

Something of the master builder rose to the surface in Jack Bull. The dugout was going to be deep and wide enough to hold us, our horses and their forage, and a rock and mud chimney. This meant much sweaty labor before any comfort could be had.

I gathered rocks for the chimney when not digging. The

hillsides were rocky and angled steeply, impossible terrain for plowing. Under the bare trees I scrambled about, hefting stones and inspecting them for weight and flatness. My compact dimensions allowed me to easily crawl under cockspur bushes and sticker weeds if a good chimney piece was beneath them. A few scratches showed up on my face but it was fun. The truth of it is, it was fun to be building something.

All of us dug hard and blistered and heehawed at joking comments. By the end of the second day we had worked off a bunch of our jumpy attitudes and were feeling calmed by the effort.

Jack Bull, with his fingers at his chin, paused often to stare at our ever-growing hole, then would begin to pace off lines and shapes, but he did it often and different each time. This was unsettling. He had grand plans for this ground but maybe too many of them.

"We should face south," he said. "We all know that. But the horses should be nearest the door."

"Whatever you think, Jack Bull," Clyde said. "I just can't get *enough* of this sweaty work, so you go on and feature it out right."

Holt and Clyde laughed. Laughs were the only sounds Holt had made in two days. He kept his tongue well rested.

"We will be in it for weeks," Jack Bull said, a little bit testy. "Might as well do it right. I don't see the sense in not doing it right."

"Ain't no one going to fight you on that," Clyde said. "I don't want to spend the winter sleeping in mud no more than you do."

"Good, good," Jack Bull said, his fingers at his chin again. "We can have a double door, or even two doors." He began to pace off a whole new bunch of lines, and said, "Then put in mud bunks along the walls and lay the chimney..."

All we diggers laughed and listened, and Jack Bull went on and on until we thought he made sense.

Then we built it.

It was right.

Just after sundown of the seventh day Holt came huffing into the hole, his pistol pulled. He spoke his first sentence in a week.

"Rider comin' this way. One minute off."

The dugout was finished and awful cozy. The chimney was about the best piece of work I've ever done, and the house in general was as sweet as you'd find underground anywhere. I think it raised some proud up in all of us. We were slow to leave it.

"Aw, let's go see to our visitor," Clyde said.

Once outside it was clear the rider was coming on bold. There was no slinking involved in the way it came straight at us. Moonlight shone down bright over the cold bare landscape. The soft clopclop of hooves yawned out across the valley. The horse snuffled and whinnied once, and if this rider was a Federal it had to be a general to be so open and silly in this country by night.

"It's just me," a feminine voice spoke. "Don't shoot or some dumb damn thing like that."

It was Sue Lee, the widow girl.

"Why, how do?" Jack Bull said and swept his hat off and swooped it around. "You talk nice, Mrs. Evans."

Sue Lee dropped down from her mount. She was bundled up thick in several pieces of clothes. They were all kinds of colors. She smelled good, or else the clothes smelled good, 'cause of a sudden something nearby smelled *real* good.

"I've brung you some dinner," she said. "Mr. Evans wishes me to apologize for not having sent you food sooner. The Federals have been on the move and he thought it safest not to. And don't you call me Mrs. Evans. My name is Sue Lee Shelley. It's a good one and I'm a widow now, you know, so I reckon I'll go on back to it and use it."

"Please pardon me," Jack Bull said in his most riverboat manner. I never liked this particular quality of his. "And come on in, won't you, Sue Lee?"

George Clyde held open the dirty plank door that opened over the dugout. Sue Lee stepped down into our place and Clyde said, "Evenin', ma'am."

Holt and I stood solid and watched as Clyde and Jack Bull did a terrific series of winks at each other, accompanied by the sneaky slinging of elbows. All it took was a girlish widow with a bucket of grub to drop by and those boys commenced to preening like there would be some huggy waltzes to be danced.

"I'll look to the horse," Holt said to me.

I still did not move. I was not much used to women except for mothers. Everything I did, they did different. I always felt that in their presence I was expected to swim a river of mud just so they could watch and giggle, then tell me I was too filthy to be seen with once I clambered up the bank. It didn't seem like anything I had to do.

"Roedel, I'll look to the horse," Holt said again. "You'd better get on in there. Let the woman see your face and know it, too."

The nigger was grinning. He'd gotten to where he acted awful familiar even if he didn't say much. I could see that he was starting to look on me like he might look on himself. That's just what happens with close living.

"I believe I know best how to handle my personal affairs, Holt." He kept his grin lit up and he didn't move back. "Why don't you see to the lady's horse. I reckon I'll go on in and check what she brung to eat."

Hold nodded, back to his mute ways, and I went on in.

I had a feeling.

There was red throughout her cheeks. One tooth was chipped in a showy part of her smile. Her hair was this big camp of black stuff falling out all around her face. Little winter drips beaded at her nose, which was a fine, thin instrument. A pale scar went an inch or so straight down her forehead and cleaved through her brow almost over the nose. Her eyes were of this endless dark hue you've never seen before.

"My," she said, "aren't you bushwhackers the gentlemen."

We all had our hats in our hands watching her. My head felt cold. An insensible bit of manners, that hat business in winter.

"We try to make the effort when possible," Jack Bull said. There was a brightness to his eyes viewing this woman. Our social life had been for a good while restricted to men, and the novelty of this widow girl being in our dugout had him glowing. "Do you think manners should be dropped in times like these, Sue Lee?"

I answered that question in my own mind right quick and hung my hat back on my head, the only spot where it did me any good.

"No," she said. Sue Lee sat on a blanket with her legs folded beneath her. She did this thing where her hand went raking soft through her hair. To me it had the aspect of a cat clawing after fleas, though I reckon it was meant to come off as coy. "But I don't think horse sense ought to be dropped either. It's cold."

Hats were slapped back on heads.

"Hmmm," went Jack Bull, a smile creeping slowly into his face. If he'd had a moustache, he would have given it a dashing tug or two. I don't know where he picked up this paddlewheel rogue approach but he seemed to think it a devastating one. "You are so kind to think of us, ma'am."

She displayed her chipped tooth then and gawked downward, and by that gesture you knew she was yet a girl in some ways despite being a widow.

"You men think of us more," she said sincerely. "You do the good work. I know it's dirty and dangerous."

I crouched back in my corner of the dugout and used the satchel of captured mail as a stool. I had carried the letters all summer long, as no good reason to dump them had hit me. It was the only gift my comrades had ever done to me and I suppose that is why I hoarded them.

"Those are good words to hear," George Clyde said. His sturdy person was squatted just to the right of the girl. "It's not always we hear them."

The bucket of grub had not been touched. It was boiled potatoes with wet bacon and corn bread for variety. I didn't feel like going through the test of eating in front of a widow who might find my table manners unique. I used to eat right, and dab my lips with a cloth after every grease dribble and hardly ever shove a potato into my mouth whole. But I had got shed of that style and did not want to hear any bad appraisals of the one I had adopted.

"Well, now," Sue Lee said, "I should be going. Mr. Evans will worry if I don't."

"Oh, ma'am," said Jack Bull. "I am awful sorry about Jackson, Junior, getting killed."

"We all suffer," she said. "But he suffers no more."

"I once met him and he was a fine boy."

"Yes," she said wistfully. She pushed up from the ground in a strong, springy way. "He was a good husband to me. For six weeks he was a good husband to me, but he didn't last."

While Jack Bull did this consoling sort of stare into her face, the door creaked open and in came Holt. He was slapping away at himself to warm up.

"What is *he* doing here?" Sue Lee asked.

"Oh, ma'am," George Clyde said, "this nigger's with me. His name is Holt. He just about don't talk at all."

A severe expression was on her face. There were not too many nigger rebels, although I had seen two others. It was a new one on her.

"He ought to be off in a field plowing with a team of other niggers," she said. "This is *our* revolution."

Clyde hooted and said, "Oh, I would reckon not, ma'am. No, ma'am. That's one nigger I wouldn't try to hitch behind a plow." He snorted and slapped standing Holt on the knee. "Holt's one nigger I wouldn't try that on."

Holt just stood there and so did the widow.

"He comes in right handy," Jack Bull said.

"Well, now," Sue Lee said dazedly. "It looks like we're going to win the fight and lose the war."

The corner of the dugout nearest the horses was Holt's, and he went over there and sat down. He sat with his legs split before him and piled his five or six pistols in between them and got real interested in how the guns looked and felt.

The widow started for the door then, and I studied the way her legs worked. She took a stride in the same fashion a man did. There was no sort of itty-bittyness to her step at all. The Evans family were aristocrats, and she had married up the hill from her own kin. That was plain. I could not picture this girl gushing beneath a pink parasol on any kind of springtime occasion.

This did not hurt her in my eyes.

"Oh, yes," she said and jumped her hand to her throat in a startled move. "I almost forgot. Mr. Evans asks that you come to the house tomorrow after dark. He is up on the Federal movements and could post you on them."

"Why, we'd be honored," Jack Bull said. "Will you be joining us?"

She squinted at him briefly, then said, "Of course. There

will be food." She then laughed pleasantly. "I haven't trained myself to go without food."

"Look forward to it, then," Jack Bull said.

All of us men joined her in standing, including Holt, who did not face her.

"I am not sure about him," she said and nodded toward Holt. "Mr. Evans has had a number of bad things in his life these past two years. A nigger with guns at the dinner table might just break his health all the way. I don't know."

"You got nothing to worry about on that score," George Clyde said. What good manners he had were beginning to be strained. "You needn't worry about Holt." Clyde had gone plain-faced. "I'll be taking him with me over to the Willards tomorrow. We won't be coming to your dinner."

"Mr. Clyde," she said. "I didn't mean to speak ill of your nigger."

"He's not my nigger. He's just a nigger who I trust with my life every day and night." George Clyde was one of the devoutest killers on the border, and there couldn't be too many sweet spots in his makeup. But Holt was one and I understood it. "I trust Holt. That's all. And it has never been a mistake."

The red in her cheeks turned up a shade and she did that flea grab at her hair again.

All I knew of Clyde and Holt was the rumor that Holt had been owned by the farmer next to Clyde's place, and that they had been boys together. The way it was said to have happened is, in the early days of the war a squad of Unionists had come sneaky-style to arrest Clyde but Holt tipped him off. When the fray commenced Holt pitched in with Clyde and afterward they were outlawed in tandem.

"That's very high praise," she said.

Clyde crossed his arms on his chest and bobbed his chin.

"Yes, ma'am. Yes it is. Praise don't get no higher."

"I see," she said. A bashful cough gave the excuse for her head to move, and she coughed it in Holt's direction. She couldn't help herself. She had to take a better look at him. Holt stood so that he offered her a steady view of the back of his hat. She scanned it quickly, then coughed herself into facing forward again. "Well, gentlemen, I really must take your leave. I hope the food will please you."

"It looks wonderful," I said.

This got her to look at me. She had not previously found my visage too terrific and still did not, but she flung a great big smile my way that put the cats to scratching in my belly.

"You are not a complainer," she said, and that great big smile shrunk. "This is not a time for complainers."

"No, ma'am," I said, as brilliant a retort as I could conjure on the instant.

"I admire you for that," she said. Her tone of speaking was plain and right at you. Most of the giggly girl squeaking had been bleached from it. "But we'll try for a better meal tomorrow anyhow. I hope to send out some pork in the morning."

"You are thoughtful, Sue Lee," Jack Bull put in. This landed him back in the window with her and her whole face straightened up at his and I could tell that the ridiculous riverboat style he had was working.

"Thank you, Jack Bull. May I call you Jack Bull?"

"I would have it no other way."

"Good. Well, I'll have Honeybee"—she held her palm facedown and halfway to the floor—"she's this *little young* girl at the house—I'll have her bring out the food if I can't come."

"That would do fine."

"Good night all," she called out, and Jack Bull jumped ahead of her to open the door. The man was fixing to be endless in his efforts to charm her down. That was clear as cow patties on a snowbank.

"Good night," I said.

"So long," said Clyde, who still sulked a smidgin.

Jack Bull halted and sucked himself up as tall as he could get, which was plenty.

"Holt," he said, "the lady said good night to all. Say good night back."

"Hey, Chiles," Clyde said hotly. "You don't tell him nothing!"

"He is being rude."

"If he needs telling, *I'll* tell him. You don't tell him nothing!"

"Then tell him, Clyde!"

"Oh, gentlemen, please!"

"He don't need telling, Chiles!"

Holt saved our association by facing about and saying, "It's okay, George." He touched his fingers to his hat brim. "'Night, missy."

Jack Bull and Clyde kept staring hard at each other and the widow lingered a look on them, then turned and started pushing at the door. This brought Jack Bull to, and he opened it and stepped outside with her.

"I'll see her to her horse," he said and closed the plank behind him.

The hot thoughts were still visible in Clyde's expression.

"Holt," he said, "you never have to be meek if I'm around."

No attitude of any sort was in Holt's face, which was always the way. He looked the same in a hot spot as he did sleeping. Anything he thought hardly ever made it to where it showed.

"It weren't no hardship, George."

I did a duckwalk over to the grub bucket and bowed my head close to it and oversniffed to draw attention my way.

"Let's eat," I said. "There's plenty for all. Smells good."

Clyde squatted into his corner and said nothing, but Holt joined me at the grub bucket and said, "It does. It surely does."

I drove a mess of potatoes into my mouth. I wrapped a string of bacon around a corn-bread chunk and set it chasing after the potatoes. The race to my gullet was more or less a tie.

Jack Bull had only stayed out a minute. He and Clyde picked at their food and were silent. Holt and me took up the slack and just slammed away the grub.

"Holt," Jack Bull said after a bit. "Do you want my bacon?"

"I could eat more," Holt said. He was starting to flourish in the chatter business.

"Good." Jack Bull got up and walked over and dropped a

nice meaty bacon string on Holt's plate. It was a meaty bacon string that would have usually been mine. I made no complaint.

" 'Preciate it," Holt said.

Clyde watched all of this and his face relaxed a good deal. He chewed away with his big jaw muscles throbbing. Pretty soon he looked my way and said, "Roedel, you want *my* bacon?"

I was full, but his gesture could not be scorned. I would have to tough down another dose of bacon for peace.

"I guess I could eat it."

Clyde smiled, and his face broke up in good cheer.

"Well, I'll shit it behind the oak tree in the morning. You just help yourself."

The dugout filled with laughter at this, and I felt fine about that, for we needed each other more and more in those times and laughter binds.

"I'll do that," I said. "Beware of my stew at noon."

The choicest part of a new day is the first of it. Despite the loitering chill of night, I squatted on the mound above the dugout and observed the great smiley head of the sun drool light into the country.

A quiet man could watch a deer shuffle by at that hour. A noisy man might startle the beast and set it bounding. A hungry man could kill it. At such a time all possibilities exist. It is a matter of choice.

My nostrils were opened by the cold and drained my head of night fluids. I snuffled and wiped and inhaled and spit. At this lonely hour I amused myself with all manner of runoffs from my person.

The peace was stunning and the creep of light, across the fallow fields and stands of timber, a revelation.

Many haunts roosted between my ears. They murmured, they pleaded, they scolded. So much echo did they unleash that I supposed myself to be diseased. I laughed out loud at things that never happened. My whole young body cringed at the briefest memory of things that had.

Among all my tormentors my father was taking the lead. He was nosing out even Asa Chiles in the provocation of unwelcome reveries. What a stubborn and luckless man he had been.

I had done what I'd done.

Was it my concern?

9

"THEY RUN ABOUT all over the country," Jackson Evans said. His old yellowing eyes swiveled to the window and saw darkness. Part of a white beard hung off his chin, but there were bare spots on his cheeks. "Waverly, Lexington, Warrensburg, all are thick with invaders." Everything about this man was long: long bony fingers, great stovepipe legs, and arms that matched an eagle span. "Would that we could drive them away, but we can't."

Dinner had shown up and been whipped good. Not a corn kernel or chicken wing survived. Thus soothed, we gathered in the parlor and went after a stout portion of apple brandy.

"We may yet," Jack Bull said. "Many of them are finding that we exact a high price from invaders. They may not want to pay it endlessly."

"No," Evans said. He shook his head. "No." This man had lost and lost to where defeat seemed a logical future. "They are too many, Mr. Chiles. They are too many, and too fanatic to quit."

The parlor had a few pieces of furniture in it. Evans had

not yet been completely robbed. As a man of significance in this neighborhood he had been offered a deal by the occupation troops. He had been roughed up some and threatened a lot, but so far he lived. Until they had proof of his traitorous thoughts, they tolerated him. He walked on a thin rail between his true sentiments and survival.

"We have different thoughts," Jack Bull said. He was as slicked-up as you could get living in a dugout. All the dirt had been plowed from beneath his fingernails, and we had took turns ranching the ticks from each other's head. The mud had been carved off our boots and we looked nigh on to dandy. "We still want to fight. I reckon I will always want to fight them."

All the women were in the other room lest we talk too terrible in front of them. They had seen terrible, and maybe felt it, but Evans clutched at old ways even amidst the awful new.

"Do not misread me, sir," Evans said. "I have given a son to this fight and would give more if I had them. No, that should not be doubted."

Jack Bull knocked back some brandy and pursed his lips. His eyes went to the floor, then to Evans.

"You have been trying to walk the neutral line, Mr. Evans, and it won't bear walking in this war."

"I know it," the old beaten gent said. "Your father, good old Asa, he tried it, too. But it don't bear walking, as you have said."

The mention of Asa doused us with a slop of gloom. He had been one of Missouri's finest, but that had not saved him, or his property, or his family.

"My father trusted the Yankees," Jack Bull said. "It is a mistake he made only once, but that was all she wrote." Jack Bull jerked himself up and began to pace. "You and him, Evans, why did you trust Yankees?"

Evans turned his hands up at this and glanced at all the night the window showed. This was tender territory with us all.

"You know why. Not because we were fools. It was because we were *not* fools. They promised us all—they called us 'prominent landowners'—they promised us we would not be bothered. They would protect us and our slaves from Jayhawkers if we pledged neutral." A whole ripple of shakes went through his form. "It made all kinds of sense at the time."

"And none now," Jack Bull said. "They didn't even protect my father from their own men. They murdered him for his watch and his boots and his horse. That is murder for cheap. And he had not taken up arms against them."

"That was the deal," Evans said. His long fingers went to picking at his beard. There was sorrow in his every gesture. "Who killed Asa, Mr. Chiles? I never knew who killed him."

"It was Captain Warren and his miserable gang. They were seen. Did you ever see Captain Warren?"

"No."

"He had a face so like that of a pig that you blinked and rubbed your eyes at the sight of him. The only excuse for a man to look so like a pig was that you were asleep and had eaten a wrong thing at dinner." The paces picked up and Jack Bull went from wall to wall. "Warren followed my

father from town and robbed him on the road. He didn't
need to kill him but he did."

"We pressed charges," I said. The recollection of us trying
to press murder charges on a Federal filled me with humilia-
tion. "They laughed at us."

"That is their habit," Evans said.

"Jake and me"—Jack Bull stopped and looked my
way—"there is always Jake with me—went for him on our
own hook. Warren had a wife. We put rags in her mouth
and met him in his very own house. I never abuse women,
but I put a quilt over her and sat on it 'til he came in."

"Well, all the rules are gone with men of that sort," Evans
said. "Their women aren't much better."

"I know it," Jack Bull said. "I liked it that way. I liked
using his wife as a chair. She was soft. It was no hard thing to
do. Captain Warren came in for vittles and got served a bitter dish. His world went sour on him. We killed him. We
killed him several times, eh, Jake?"

"That's right," I said. "There was no chance left in it."

"It was our first real fight. Everything got changed by it."

"You took to the bush," Evans said. "All the good men are
in the bush now."

"Those are words that have went south forever," Jack Bull
said. "'Good' doesn't mean anything like what it used to
mean. No, sir, we are not *good* men. But we are men. They'll
have to whip us. We won't do it for them by quitting."

"My prayers are with you," Evans said. "They have become
more frequent, and they are always with you men in the
bush." Evans stared off and breathed sadly. He had once been

a man best left unmolested, but now he was old. "We will be quitting this country in the spring. As soon as the roads are clear we will be trying for Texas."

"About half of Missouri has went to Texas," I said. "Plenty of friends are there."

Evans nodded my way, and a thin, unhappy smile broke from him.

"Yes," he said. "It is about the only place left. This land is ruined."

Jack Bull splashed out some more brandy, and silence dropped down. I held the brandy up and studied it as if it might tell me much. Beaten old men were not the right philosophers for young straight-backed boys, who would trade shots and victories, to hear. I watched the liquor so my glance needn't pause at the aged, whipped face of our host.

"What of the Federals?" I asked to chase off the sorrowful quiet. "What are they doing?"

"Ah," said Evans. He crouched forward as if intent on me, and his movements creaked. "The militia has taken up your tactics. Iowans and so forth will guard the towns and the militia will meet you in the bush."

"They have been trying that," Jack Bull said. "It hasn't been their best trick."

"They say it will be. There are plenty of them." Evans pointed a finger that aimed somewhere between where Jack Bull stood and I sat. "This Quantrill man, this man who sails under the name of Captain Quantrill, has them hornet-angry. He kills and kills. They want his head on a pole."

"I shouldn't wonder at that," I said. "He has lots of boys and they are rough."

"Do you know Quantrill?"

"Yes," Jack Bull said. "We have joined up with him for a couple of things. His ideas work."

"I believe he is trash," Evans said. "I believe that even if he is on our side."

A kind of deadly bored look worked into Jack Bull's face.

"I would watch that talk, Mr. Evans," he said. "The boys love him. He leads well. He may truly be trash. Maybe you would not have spoken to him five years ago, but those days are gone, sir. Trash that fights mean now make up the best men on the border."

Jackson Evans nodded at this, as though changed by hearing it, then set down his brandy and pulled himself upright. It was a long process.

"Enough of this war talk," he said. "Let's have the ladies join us and think nobler thoughts."

"A fine idea," Jack Bull said with gusto. "Some company would be splendid."

Old Evans cranked his feet up to the pace of a scared turtle, and creaked off through the house to call in the women. This hobnobbing in the midst of war had the quality of fevered thought. It did not fit at all. It was happy memories acted out in forlorn surroundings. There was sentiment in such gestures, like saving the first spoon that was jammed in your mouth as a babe. The thing didn't fit anymore, and knowing that it once had was no great joy.

"Jack Bull," I said. I stood to shake my legs loose. "We should be thinking about getting on back. Federals could pass any time."

"Oh, put a gown on, Jake." He laughed at my concerns.

"It is too cold. They'll all be in front of the fire examining their plunder."

The women and the girl joined us. Mrs. Evans was a wide cart of mother with a florid face and blond hair. She wore spectacles. Her chin had extras hanging below it. I liked her on sight. She pleased the eye and heart almost as well as my own mother, or Missus Chiles, could have.

Sue Lee's hair had been reined in a bit. She went right at the brandy and poured herself a dollop. Allowances were made for women as well as men in such times.

"I have it in me to sing," she said. "Shall we have a sing-along?"

This Honeybee creature was a seedling version of her mother, destined to grow wide and strong and pleasing.

"Oh, yes," she said. "I like those the best."

"My voice is not all it should be these days," Jack Bull said, "but once it was rumored I could carry a tune."

This was all too much for me. Sing-alongs were the main attraction at socials my whole life, and I never did like them. It could be that I sang without tone or spirit or joy. My voice had an ability to hit and founder at several odd depths in any one chorus.

"I believe I won't sing," I said. "Young ears are present."

The widow girl sliced a look at me that was meant to drag me along into song.

"I'll bet you sing lovely," she said.

"You would lose."

"He really does sing very poorly," Jack Bull said. "He imitates the turkey first-rate, though."

He was peddling his social graces hard at my expense. I didn't even want the widow.

Honeybee took my hand, as is the forward style of lonely country tykes.

"Would you do a gobble for me, sir?" she asked.

I rubbed Honeybee's soft little head, then grabbed her by the shoulders and spun her 'til she faced in another direction.

"It is too cold, Honeybee," I told her. "When I call turkeys—they come. They would come all a-gobble and crash right through those windows and we would freeze."

"Oh," she said, pouty, and I shoved her off toward her mother. "I want to hear it. I want you to gobble, sir."

"Catch me in better weather."

I guess I amused the widow, as she smiled at me in a tiny lip-curl fashion that I supposed indicated minute mirth.

Mrs. Evans put her arms around Honeybee and held her to her tummy.

"Don't pester the man so," she said. "We're going to sing, Honeybee. You like to sing, don't you?"

"If he won't gobble, I'll sing." The wide-woman seedling smoldered a look at me. "He don't care for me."

This banter with a child was tightening me up. The social whirl was not my form of tumult. All my stabs at it missed the mark.

"I like you fine," I said. "It's just gobbling right now is not for me."

Soon the crowd got over my not gobbling and started singing. They beat through "Dixie" and "Barbry Allen," then worked over "Kiss Me Katie Oh." Old Evans honked out the low parts and Jack Bull stretched up after notes that he fumbled gamely and the women sang in the soothing center range.

Brandy was sloshed around.

I leaned against a wall and smiled constantly, like an addlebrain.

It pretty well made me jumpy, hooting out songs in a secesh house in a Federal district. I had not the same capacity for convincing myself that I was elsewhere from where I was. I knew exactly where I was and it wasn't a place for songs.

Aw, pretty quick I said the devil with it all and went outside. I tried to keep a watch and the moon helped some by throwing that weak light down on the road. I could sort of see a good distance and that relaxed me.

The night chill had routed any ragtag pockets of heat. My nose burned. Water beaded in my eyes. A granny thing happened to my hands and they could barely clinch. I hopped about inside a blanket and crashed my hat down around my ears.

Inside the house the sing-along went on. Jack Bull Chiles would have us killed for a widow squeeze and a chance to mangle high notes in company. The voices were muffled by the walls and wind and reached my ears all souped together.

In every way, and for as many reasons, I wanted to return to the mud dugout and my rock chimney.

But if Jack Bull Chiles ever was hurt because I left him, there would be no recovery for me. I knew that. I had always known that. It was something that I knew from toenail to cowlick.

So I watched the road and blew on my hands and stamped my feet and damn near froze, but no bad luck gained on us.

It was as pleasant a night as I'd had in a while.

10

IN THE COMING days the widow found daily missions that required her presence in our dugout. George Clyde was often at Juanita Willard's and sometimes Holt was at his side. Sometimes he was left in the dugout. Sue Lee got friendlier and more sisterly to Holt and me. Jack Bull would not be mistaken for her relative by any but the most backward sort of person.

Really, she quit seeming like a widow. She seemed like a seventeen-year-old girl from Carthage, Missouri, which is what she was. When Jack Bull started putting her paw in his, she fell for the ploy. She liked that gambit. It had worked on her before, I think.

One day when the snow had fallen, she hustled into the dugout and bellowed a howdy, which had become her greeting. Two balls of snow were in her hands. She hurled one at me but missed and splattered Holt. The other she walked over and rubbed in Jack Bull's face. He never even moved to avoid it, but held his face up and open to her fingers and the cold they mashed all about his features.

"You splattered poor Holt," I said to her. "Your aim is wild."

"It surely is," she answered. The snow was melting on my near brother's face. He looked like the boy who has been scolded only to discover that the right scolding can be a pleasant business. She turned from him and looked on Holt. "Did I whop you good?"

As was his wont, Holt merely nodded.

The whole long fence of her teeth went on display. She was frisky and happy and wallowing in her mood, as only someone who does not often feel it will. She went over and shoved Holt.

"Holt," she said, giggling. "I'll make you speak up one of these days."

He looked up at her and laid his head off to one side.

"Don't hold your breath, missy."

This one sentence delighted her. She busted up harder with mirth than you would at several Shakespeares.

"I have done it!" she cried. "I have made old Holt talk!"

Love must be what it was. This mood just crashed right out of her and slammed around the dugout. I thought, It must be akin to a terrible fever, only it races happy through you and not heat. Maybe there is some heat, too. It is a sight to watch if you ain't got it yourself.

Jack Bull stared at her kind of sheepish, and she kept giddying about 'til he said, "Whoa, mule! Settle down, there."

Calling a lovestruck girl a mule in company is not a winning comment. I learned that quick by the way Sue Lee's face twitched straight from giddy to grumpy. She turned a look on Jack Bull that showed plain that she saw no great compliment in the comparison.

"Mule?" she said. "Whoa, mule?"

There was snowmelt trickling over his face, and he wiped at it. He looked my way as if I might relay him a good lie that would slide him out of this.

"Just calm down," he said.

She leaned over so her face was just above him. She pinched her cheeks and said, "Do I look muley to you?"

"Well, no."

Then she did this thing that I would have plunked down five cents to see if I hadn't gotten it free. She spun about, put her hands on her knees and sashayed her butt practically into his surprised nose. Despite her many garments the movement showed some charms.

"That look like a mule to you?" She stood straight while he looked stupid, then she did it again. He took his punishment well. "That look like the rear end of an animal that heehaws in the night?"

Jack Bull smiled at that and dug himself in deeper.

"It looks like it might could be."

I am afraid Holt and me laughed. We were always loitering in the midst of their carrying-ons. Romance is a sweet enough enterprise but it makes you lonely to watch it. Holt grinned at me and I sent the same back to him.

"Jack Bull Chiles," Sue Lee said, "just because I'm a widow it don't mean you can get that familiar with me."

"Pardon me, ma'am, but I believe it was you that shoved your rump into my face."

"Oh!" she went. "That was only just to make a point!"

"You made it," he said. He could be rough at the oddest

moments. "I will always know your rump from a mule's now. There are several differences. I don't know how I missed them."

Now, Sue Lee Shelley was not the sort of plantation belle that would be contented by a mere exchange of rhyming insults. She came of practical people in a practical land. She smote him a good one on the chin.

Twice in my life I had also taken swings on Jack Bull, and her blows shook him even less than mine had. She wound up to fling another at him, but he sprang to his feet and grabbed her in close to him. His arms were all around her.

My Lord, Holt and me wanted out of that dugout. Some things you ought not to ever see your best friend do up close. Love is one of them. Me and Holt went dirt-quiet and faced every way but their way.

"Don't be mean," she said, and this time she sounded about twelve years old and lost. "I can't tolerate meanness."

There was some breathy silence, then wet noises were made and several sighs accompanied them. I have a fragment of the gentleman in me, but I ditched it and looked over my shoulder at all the friendliness. Jack Bull was doing some moist mouth work on her neck and cheeks and lips. He nuzzled her all about. Pretty soon she was doing similar deeds on him.

He had a slit-lidded look on him. His arms kept her in the hug and all those noises went on.

In peacetime he might have been shot for this.

"Is that too mean?" he finally asked.

"No," she answered in a tiny tone. "It's not really *too* mean at all."

I guess a woman wants a man in wartime. While there still are any. People in hell want springwater.

Holt found all kinds of fascinating aspects to the dirt between his feet. He knew he better not look anywhere else. A nigger's path is awful narrow when white women are around.

This big huggy smooching match changed the dugout. It happened in a blink. There I was squatting on the dirt with Holt, feeling just about as useful as a Christian impulse at an ambush, while Jack Bull kept up at his new sport of mashing on widows. It seemed he found this new game to be less than heroically difficult.

I about screamed.

But finally the widow showed some sense. She crawdad-died out of his arms. A couple of satisfied humphs came from her as she patted herself back into place. Then she said, "Oh, goodness."

"Yes," he said, and his tone was exactly that of a faro dealer who knows the game ain't straight. "Goodness is what it is."

"Aw, for crying out loud!" I said. I pointed at hunkered Holt, then myself. "We're sitting right here! Show us some mercy."

My comments had a stunning effect. All the mushy stuff went up the chimney. I didn't glance to see it, but I could feel Jack Bull staring hard at me. No one knew him better, or even as well.

"He is quite right," Sue Lee said. "I must leave. I have to get. I better get to the house."

"Cover your tracks in the snow, too," I said. "You'll be leading curious Federals right onto us."

"Now, don't be rude," Jack Bull said. "You have no reason to be rude."

I faced him after that.

"Is that so?" I asked. I could display some pesky qualities myself when forced to it. "There is a war going on everywhere but between your ears, you dumb ox."

I guess I was more than pesky.

He kicked me square in the chest. I felt my innards bobble. The next few breaths I drew rattled and wheezed.

"Dumb ox, am I?"

Oh, he had that look for a moment there. It was not the look I most liked to see. But it passed as fast as it came.

"I'm sorry, Jake," he said. I think he meant it. "My leg just did that on its own. There was no thought behind it."

I rubbed and rubbed at the place where his boot had visited all on its own. It was a dull throbbing spot.

"I hear you," I said. "I hear you. These things happen. But Holt and me ain't dying just so you can be kissed."

"Leave me out of this," Holt bleated. "I ain't even here, or nowhere near here."

Jack Bull laughed. His eyes had a lantern glow.

"I don't believe anyone is about to die from my kiss. In fact, she seems to be doing tolerably well."

The widow excused herself swiftly. She got right out of there. I reckon widows feel okay about acts that some maidens might drown themselves over. Anyhow that's the way I figured it.

When she was gone Jack Bull said, "Hey, looky here, boys."

"Where?" I asked.

"Right here."

There was a big lump in his britches square between where his pistols hung.

"My God," I said. "Where's your shame, Chiles?"

"Gone to Texas," he said, and just uproared with lewd joy.

I couldn't chime in.

Nothing was the same.

The chimney fire broke light across the dugout. It was a jagged illumination. The flames writhed and bounced and a deathly howl of wind blew down the chimney. It felt homey to me.

George Clyde was back. He was ruining Juanita Willard's reputation. Often he stayed with her all night. Her family seemed to think nothing of it. If ever we won the war, it would take years to renovate our honor. Honor had come to be a frivolous virtue in practice, but it was also the one that urged us to battle.

Confusing.

"So, now," Clyde said to Jack Bull. "You have become quite the young swain, I hear."

"I can't deny it."

"You have been loose with your kisses, I hear."

"Not as loose as I hope to be."

"Hah, hah! I know that feeling." Clyde, by dint of his regular berth at the Willards, seemed practically married. "What is she like?"

"Oh, she is fine. Just fine and dandy. A robust widow."

"Those are by far the best kind," Clyde said. "And there are getting to be plenty of them."

This conversation seemed two-sided, so I threw in my own oar.

"She is coltish of attitude," I said. "With an ungainly gallop of spirit."

"Ho, ho," went Clyde. "You are making me jealous!"

Jack Bull beamed. He chewed at a twig, his strong cheeks bulging around a smile. His skin seemed flushed to about the same degree as six chugs of popskull whiskey would do.

"Yes," he said. "This gal is *some* proposition."

"She is lowly born," I said.

"Oh, she is. She is lowly born," Jack Bull said happily, "but highly fascinating."

Clyde went to giggling and said, "Leave off with it—you boys are making me *so* jealous."

"I say again," Jack Bull mused. "She is lowly born but highly fascinating."

I felt wounded and left by the roadside.

Change was required of me.

I didn't know if I was up to it.

Things got worse. George Clyde had Juanita Willard beg Sue Lee to come stay with her, and Clyde drug Jack Bull over there the next night. That left Holt and me in the dugout. The two of them set out like it was a lark. All kinds of backslapping and winking went on.

I hoped they were shot at, but not hit.

Maybe they could be hit just slightly.

It was kind of glum for me in the dugout. It was awful cold out. Winter is mostly melancholic. It is especially so underground.

Holt was barely more company than a rock. He had to be coaxed and goaded to say "Pass the taters." I was not exactly windy of nature myself, but I wanted some conversation.

"Pick a topic," I said.

He just looked at me, his black skin blacker in the poor-lighted corner.

"Pick a topic," I chorused. "You are going to talk to me, Holt."

His head shook, and his hands flinched and he said, "It's not my habit."

Everything he said he said fine enough, but he didn't seem to believe it. Actually he said things as good as anybody. A lot of niggers I had known blathered hoodoo nonsense to where you wanted to gag them, but here I was, alone, with a well-spoken nigger who had a terrible case of silence. It is always something.

"I'll pick the topic," I finally said. I had to lure this fellow into conviviality. I tried to think of some topic we could both discuss. I didn't want it one-sided. "Let's talk about— dirt. Dirt is our topic."

When he still failed to respond, I began to suspect that he was not bashful but ornery.

"Dirt, damn it, Holt. Tell me all you know about dirt."

He looked at me. His eyes were shaded toward the oriental in shape. I don't think I impressed him at all.

"Dirt is good," he said. For no more exercise than it got, his tone was rich. "Everywhere is dirt. Dirt is good."

"Well, now, that's dandy," I said. "It's just you and me here, Holt. We need to talk or we'll be crazed by the wind moans."

There was some suspicion in me that Holt found my company comfortable. It was a slow thing with him, friendliness was. Somewhere in him I felt there was a great goo of warmth that he stored slyly.

"Is that all you know of dirt?" I asked. A long response would not have pained me.

"It is dark," he said. You could parade his voice at a song-fest and not get hooted. It was that pleasant. "Do you think George will marry?"

"Not in these times," I said. "After this war is gone, he will. I reckon we'll all have to."

"Aha," he hummed. "The trick is us passing through these times."

Holt was a sensible creature with opinions that were succinct. I could not fail to note it.

"Just so," I said.

Well, we stared at the shadows on the walls for a spell to regain our breath after such a spurt of chat. It looked like cities. The shadows peaked and valleyed all across the dugout and for flashes of time they designed out tall buildings and great avenues that resembled precisely no city I'd ever heard of, but they diverted nonetheless.

"There is something I like," Holt said. His smart face straightened at me.

"Oh, what would that be?"

"You might not care for it, Roedel."

"Try me. I can be generous when the cost is low."

He studied me closely, then said, "You ain't the same as some of the boys. I have watched you. It's a thing I have seen."

"How nice of you to like that," I said.

"That ain't it. Not what I like." An expression very like that of an unfed puppy was on him. It had its endearing aspects. "I like it when you read."

"Read what?"

"The mails. When you read them mails out loud it is something the likes I never heard before."

The mail pouch was baggage I toted the same way others rub quartz rocks—it was part of my luck. I knew I'd had some to be yet nearly whole. But I had not read the letters. That might not be something that should be done.

"Oh, they might not be too amusing," I said. "It might just be a bunch of boring thoughts one stranger sent to another."

This comment made him look down. He brushed dust from his britches and stared away from me.

"The one you read from the mother was fine," he said. "I heard that from you in the spring. Do you recall it?"

"Yes."

"She said things I enjoy to hear."

There was nothing for it but to read. Jagged flame and the shadows it throws can be amusing for only a while. A letter might almost be as fine as a conversation.

I pulled out the mail pouch. I opened the flap and held it toward Holt.

"Draw one, Holt."

His fingers inched into the pouch and he felt around a bit, as if the feel of the note could sway him yea or nay. After some seconds of tactile scrutiny he drew one out.

"This one do," he said.

I opened the letter. It was a Massachusetts scrawl of a thing. Half of rabid Kansas had come from there with the Emigrant Aid Society. They shipped abolitionists and Bibles and rifles out to our area to stir up trouble. It was hard to like them. This letter was addressed to Andrew Pritchard in Lawrence, Kansas, the most hated burg on the border, home of the Jayhawkers and their foam-mouthed ilk.

"You are some picker," I said. I about did not read it, for I knew the author of it would insult me from a distance. "Okay, here goes...."

I belted out the contents of the Yankee thing. It developed that father Pritchard in Wellfleet, Massachusetts, was very proud of young Andrew for having the pluck to come out to our territory and try to force us into being more like them. It is war to the knife and knife to the hilt, he said, which is exactly the same way we saw it. God's will must be done, he said, and rebels had sacrificed the right to the love of any known God, for he didn't imagine that the God he prayed to in Massachusetts could possibly stomach Missouri men.

Well, I thought, this man follows a frail deity.

"I don't want to read this," I said. "It is making me forlorn, the stinginess of it. Draw out another."

"I am with you," Holt said, as he dipped his fingers into the pouch. "I want to hear nice things, and that man don't say them."

"You have got that right." The new letter was folded into a tiny square. I opened it slowly. "Holt, where is your mother?"

"Aw, Kansas or Kingdom. I don't know which."

I could tell this was something he thought of often. Anybody would. Sad deeds were done in this land. I never owned a nigger or even bid on one.

"Well, my father is murdered," I said, as I undid the tiny square.

"I know that," he said. "George's whole family is murdered. Even his momma, who was not too well anyhow."

"Does Clyde own you?"

His head shook, his lips turned down.

"Not in greenbacks and coppers," he said.

"I see," I said, and I did.

The tiny square unfolded to reveal a big sloppy script. It, too, was from Massachusetts and en route to Lawrence. This one was from a brother to a brother. A real hardy tone was in it. The back-east brother had seen a theatrical in Boston where an Englishman played Othello with bootblack so effectively smeared on his face that he fully expected John Brown's ghost to waft in and double the ticket price. These boys were named Fannin. The letter writer went on to say that so many niggers were now freed and in Boston that Irishmen could hardly get jobs on the docks. He allowed as how this was not a phenomenon that had been predicted by the Black Republicans, but it was one he was having to live with. He then said he loved his brother and he often thought warmly of him and the times when they had missed the shape-up and gone rowing in the harbor, and the sweaty nights after they had humped on the docks all day only to dance too late at Parlan's Beer Garden. Oh, Jesus, he said, life was not so rough when your favorite brother was with you and there were droves of single gals roaming about and beer was free if they were one of Parlan's daughters. Here's to you, he finished, and keep your head low out there.

"Is this a better one?" I asked Holt.

"A good deal nicer," he said with a nod. "It could get to where you might like that man."

"Yes," I said. "In other times he would not be so bad."

What we said was true. I had barely disliked anyone before woop and warp had come my way, and never hated. But I had learned all these emotions that some call necessary and noble. I would never apologize for it, yet I might have thrived without it.

"Holt, do you reckon this war will ever end?"

"No."

"Me neither," I said. "Not unless we are killed."

"Oh, yes," he said, and patted his pistols. "That would do it. I left that out."

"You reckon we'll be killed?"

"Mmmmm," he went, and I really liked him, for a nigger. "Old men is not a way I ever figure us to be."

11

OR SEVERAL DAYS Venus ruled. The dugout became a
mere hotel for George and Jack Bull, and a dodderer's
home to Holt and me. The romance men preened themselves into oily specimens, and leaked out a roughhewn,
mocking good cheer.

They had plumbed the savory well and we had not. It
seemed to make all the difference.

Jack Bull now had private tunes that he whistled for his
pleasure only, but he still slapped me like a brother and set
aside extra time for talking to me. He was kinder in his comments than usual. That is, when he and George were not
strutting their stallion facets.

It all made my cheeks blanch. He treated me like an idiot
child and I was neither.

By the calendar it was well into January and not as cold as
it should have been. I pointed this out.

"Since it is not so cold, we should go out on a scout of
some sort. The snow is melted."

The Venus-struck pair showed no interest.

"You are a fount of bad ideas," George Clyde said. My,

how a little regular sin had changed *his* interests. "It could snap cold at any time."

Later, Jack Bull Chiles and me sat alone, sharing tales of adventures we had taken together. We talked purple improbable patches of half-right details about the sultry summer day when we had swum in the Big Muddy, then rattled the fragile citizens by loping bare-assed to home, and of the gray, crisp September day when our first deer fell before us, and similarly unimportant days that loomed large in recollection. Everybody has them. A few things we did in the wrong came up, but we refashioned those deeds with our speech and came out of them now looking fine. We turned blunders inside out and wore them as victories.

"This thing with Sue Lee," I said. "Will it go on?"

By his face and eyes I saw clear that he would not make a joke of my query.

"I would reckon," he said.

Our hair had gotten so long that I was always aware of it. We had sworn not to cut it 'til the war was won. My hands went to my long pale locks and fingered them about.

"Well, now," I said. "That is good for you."

"Yes. I believe I'll marry her."

"But she is a widow."

"What of it?" He shrugged and looked happy. "She suits me as good as I can be suited, Jake."

There was no room for churlishness on my part. I was learning to accept that I was not crucial to the turning of the world, or the turning of his world, and often not even to my own.

"Congratulations, Jack Bull," I said, dredging up all the mastery of voice I owned. "You will make the finest pair in Missouri, I can see that right now."

"She's a wonderful gal."

"She is fine in every way," I said.

"And you know," he said, a big rare smile on him, and his hand flying to pat my shoulder, "she feels the same about me! Ain't that something?"

"Oh, it really is," I said. "A big ox like you — well, I would not have predicted it."

"I know." He was so pleased that I felt overwhelmingly alone. "But she does."

"That is wonderful. You would have to eat a peach and bring it back clean to top that."

"Oh, at least. At least that."

Well, the winter wore on. Riley Crawford visited us. He had some news — evil things were winging over our country. Several comrades had gotten bold from boredom and went riding into the next world. I knew them, and it was bad to hear. Riley stayed two nights, then moved on, safely I hoped.

In what must have been late February, Turner Rawls and the Hudspeth brothers came over just to hear some different lies, they said. Turner's banged-up mouth had healed, but not right. A coin size of black torn skin had grown over the bullet hole in his cheek. His teeth did not mesh. He spoke slobber-tongued like a dog would if a dog could. It was sad, and it was plain that he thought so, too. Sometimes he would start out on a sentence, then kind of drool off the track and his eyes would water and his fingers tremble. I had come to like him so much. His affliction made me way wistful, and I would wag my nubbin in his face, trying to cheer us both.

These boys relayed the word that Black John wanted us all to rally at Captain Perdee's farm as soon as the weather broke. They were anxious to be on the prod again, and the sorrowful deaths of winter had me willing to share their mood.

A day later they left.

In very early March, a month special to me, for I was born in it, Clyde left the dugout to go to Juanita Willard's and add some details to his ruin of her reputation. Nothing was ever said of this.

Holt was left behind by Clyde. It had become the way, for Holt was merely an intrusive specter at the Willard house.

On this day I saw a three-legged buck, with battered antlers and worn fur, drag off through the woods. The proud stag lived on but, crippled up and worn, he would soon feed other beasts.

The sun was all over the sky, no clouds trifled with it. Holt, Jack Bull and me sat in front of the dugout, smelling the clean wind and staring out over all the land eyesight can survey.

In even the foulest of weather there are still several fine points of beauty to a day. But on a day as wonderful as this the marvels of our existence were everywhere to be noted, and any fault hard to find.

"Sue Lee will be by today," Jack Bull said.

"Good," I said. "It's been near a week since I've seen her."

"Yes. All this warmth has the Federals out for jaunts. That has kept her home."

"Ah, yes," I said. "It won't be long before we join them — out there."

"No, it won't," Jack Bull said. He was acting a bit more casually sincere than I knew him to be. "That is why I want to ask something of you and Holt."

"Name it."

"Well, there, future best man," he said, "I would ask you to give us some privacy."

"Oh, you would, would you?"

"It's not much to ask."

"What are Holt and me to do?"

He turned his hands up in that way that is the common response to pointless questions.

"Anything you'd like. Fling walnuts at squirrels, play mumblety-peg, study leaves. Whatever you want."

I said, "I reckon we can come up with a better use of our time than that, eh, Holt?"

"It is a possible," he said, and nodded.

It was nowhere near dark when Sue Lee arrived. She came winding along up through the woods. A few snowbanks were still there in the shadowy parts of the landscape. Over the winter she had gotten sly and never took exactly the same path to the dugout twice in a row. Her discretion in this regard was much appreciated.

When she drew near us, she said howdy in that sassy tone of hers. That tooth was still chipped in the center of her smile, and that pale scar still cleaved her brow and her hair continued to go its own way, but she had gotten much prettier to me. The hue of the rose was on her cheeks. A dose of serenity had been put to her, and the effect it had was fine and pleasing.

"I brung you two something," she said to Holt and me. One of her hands slinked under her cloak and she raised out a half loaf of fresh bread and a spoon of butter in a rag. "Try this bread, boys."

She handed the loaf to me. The scent of it was welcome. Fresh bread—you wouldn't think it could be as special as it can be when you ain't gnawed any for a spell.

"Why, thank you," I said. "Did you make it?"

"No, no," she said, and smiled. "Mrs. Evans's sister lives in the town. She is a Federal but a sister still. She gave us two loaves."

"That is kind of her. Thank her for us, won't you?"

She laughed.

"I don't suppose I'll tell her where it went. That might not do."

Jack Bull was standing at the dugout door, holding it open, impatient for his privacy. Holt ducked in and came back out with the mail pouch and a solemn expression.

"Hmmm," I said. "This good weather has me and Holt wanting to go off and fling walnuts at mumblety-peg players, or something along those lines."

"Have fun," Jack Bull said.

Sue Lee went down into the dugout. It was as much her place as anyone's now.

"Jake," Mister Romance said. He held his trigger finger up and whispered, "One hour. One hour."

I nodded to him. This all seemed like more secrecy than an obvious smoochy tryst required. But it saved us from openly mentioning things. That might lead to too many interesting opinions being flaunted.

So, as it was as splendid a day as it was, my bachelor partner and me clambered up the slope above the dugout. We threaded through the trees, walking on the stiff soil, Holt lugging our pouch of recreation.

To have this dark man around me so regular was no hardship. He grew on me. Bravery enough was in his sturdy frame to match any requirement. I had come to think that even his silences were not mute taunts but moments of reflection. And they had gotten more rare. Alone with me he gabbed plenty.

Our feet slapped on up to a log fallen sideways that had a view of the valley. We sat on it. The Evans house was off in the distance, and the chimney could be just barely seen. This was a pleasant spot to lose an hour in.

"Jake," Holt said as we sat. "I been going over this in my thoughts. In the mails the Yankee man say the rebel is a blight but not on what. To what is a rebel a blight?"

This had gotten to be our Socratic style. Holt pestered me with questions and more questions, many of which I could barely handle. He had taken hold of the notion that I was a blue-eyed, pale-haired, short-legged immigrant oracle. He was curious in several directions but was especially so about Europe and supposed that somehow I knew a great deal about it. At the least-expected time he would ask such things as, "Jake, in the other world do they do this, or that?"

If the truth were real important to me, I would need to

'fess up to the left-out detail, which was, I sort of enjoyed playing the role of a man who knew a few of the answers.

In the brightness of this day on the hillside I said, "The rebel is a blight on the Yankee man's will, Holt."

"His will?"

"Yes, his will." I was gesticulating out onto all the hills and timber, and it seemed that plenty of fox squirrels and field mice were listening and watching with astute attention. "The Yankee is this cut of man, Holt. He is the cut of man who if you say the sun is high, he will say, no, you are low. That is nothing in itself to war over. But then he will say, I believe my way and my life and person have more loft to them than yours do, so be like me." My hands were waving all about, chopping and weaving to drive home my points. If by chance a crowd had been there, I reckon they would have elected me. "The rebel is not the man you want to say that to. He don't care for it."

"I know that."

"Sure you do," I said. "And you know this, too—the rebel will fight you if you try to force him to your way. And it don't matter too much what your way is, neither."

Holt fingered his chin in a thoughtful manner. His lips bunched up.

"Is that good?" he asked.

"Holt, to me it is the best that can be said of any man—he had his convictions and he backed them up. I revel in that quality. It is so sweet an outlook that it is almost only for youngsters."

"I don't know my age," he said. "It is not too high in the numbers, I do know that."

"Mine neither. We are the perfect age for not cottoning to being invaded and shoved around."

For bachelors we were having a pleasant enough time. The sun had crept behind us, but many minutes of light were left. We had not been quite so easygoing at times over the winter. The Venus boys made us feel left back. Our flagrant bachelorhood had had us in an irritable state. We had seemed so dull that we were angered at ourselves and testy with all lovers.

But now that boat had sailed. Really, I was glad for Jack Bull Chiles and Sue Lee Shelley, as a good woman and a good man is a grand match. Only the depraved and imbeciles can deny it.

"Dark will fall," Holt said. I knew what was coming. He had that look. "I brung the mails."

"Aw, drag one out." I knocked his hat off but he caught it and put it back. "Don't act so bashful. I knew you would do this."

Reading other people's mail had taught us plenty. I did not mind doing it, for we both learned much. In Cairo, Illinois, there is a mound that gives a view of mingling rivers and that view has inspired several kisses. Ohio has a place called Chagrin Falls, where a gristmill grinds the day long and an old man just wishes his sons would come home whole and watch the flour sift out. New York is jammed with folks who are not New Yorkers and don't especially care to die in Tennessee, so they riot in the streets and blame it on niggers. Mothers are mothers all over the map. They want to send shortbread and new gloves and warm thoughts. Girl friends know all the same tricks there as here. Locks of hair are often

in their letters, along with faded flower petals and, sometimes, bad news.

Holt handed me his selection. It was a letter sent from St.
Louis to Topeka. The paper it was written on was of high
quality. I had been to St. Louis twice with Asa Chiles. There
were many stores there that peddled goods of such high
quality that they made no sense to me. A two-dollar hat sits
on the head just as well as one that cost twelve, but you saw
the twelve-dollar kind all over the street.

"Read it," Holt said. "I am in the mood to hear a good one."

"I just read them," I said. "This thing is addressed to Miss
Ruth Ann Jones and it's from a Miss Patricia Foote. 'Dearest
Ruth Ann, I trust this letter will reach you before winter.
Here it is always a sort of winter, as folks are so cold now.
The rebels are out of the city as far as armies go but crafty
Copperheads slink around performing misdeeds. So much
cruelty goes on. Gratiot Prison is full of rebels and they are
left to waste away so pitifully. They are traitors but also
human. If you looked in on them you would not believe that
they were, for they resemble scarecrows now.

"'So much death and no coffee to be had. I have made
myself forget that sugar exists, for it may as well not unless
you know Generals. Men are killed over poultry here. There,
too, I suppose.

"'I wonder, do you still favor Tennyson? John Greenleaf
Whittier seems more rare to me. Do you remember when
we studied Wordsworth at Miss Fielding's and you said his
was God's voice strained through a man? Whittier is the
same to me.

" 'Your last letter thrilled me. I hope you do marry Mr. Anthony but I believe that even in Kansas he must first ask you.

" 'There is no one here for me to marry. The men all talk too fondly of this war for me. I believe they find it much more interesting than me with my pince-nez and poetry.' "

I cut the letter off. The war was yet on, a continuous enterprise. At any time I might be forced to put my life at auction and barter the price as high as good shooting makes possible. I didn't want any flickers of goodwill toward my targets to tremble my aim.

"That's enough reading," I said. "Has it been an hour?"

"No. The hour ain't gone yet."

The bread sat on the log between us, so we ripped it up and spread butter on it with our fingers. The taste was all to the good, and the sun was skulking off behind the hills and gloom spreading before us. Holt smacked away at a bread chunk and I mimicked him.

"Do you know my name?" he asked after a noisy swallow.

"It is Holt."

"No, my whole name." His tone was low and direct. "My whole name is Daniel Holt. Daniel, like the lion's-den man. Do you know his story?"

"Of course I do," I said. "That man was in a pinch but got hisself out of it by standing tall."

"That's right. You have heard it. That's why I am named after him."

Gloom took over. The sun fled the neighborhood. Full dark swept away my vision. Coldness came up on me quick and I shivered.

"Is it an hour now?" I asked.

"Nigh on to it."

That is when we heard the first shot. The faint crack ambled to us from a distance, then several more came in a bunch.

"The Evanses' place," I said.

"Got to be."

We scrambled down the dark slope, using our hands as shields, bouncing from tree to tree to dirt and up again, sliding toward the dugout.

I jerked the rough plank door open and jumped into the room. Instantly I wished I had knocked. They lay by the fire, Jack Bull's britches around his ankles and Sue Lee's skirt covering her face.

"Gunshots at the Evanses' place," I said. Holt started in and I shouted, "Stay out, Holt!"

I faced away from the fallen. They made rustling noises and murmured.

"I heard them," Jack Bull said. "I heard them. You can turn around now."

He went to buckling his pistols on and she smiled painfully, for there was no joke prompting the expression. Her skirt covered what it ought to. She walked over to me, her cheeks all scarlet, and placed a hand on my shoulder.

"Oh, Jake," she said.

She looked on me sad—sad for me, I realized, like she believed she had just boiled down the last mess of my baby-fat illusions.

I shook her hand off.

"You stay here," I told her. "Out of the way. There's going to be a fight."

We dragged our mounts out and rode without saddles. The beasts had not been much exercised and moved sluggishly for such fine animals. We picked down the hill to a dry creek that led toward the house.

"Can you put a number to them?" Jack Bull asked.

"No," I answered. "Not too many."

The fine hand of villainy soon had light rising up where we knew the house stood. I hoped the wide cart of mother was not hurt, or little Honeybee. Jackson Evans would be in pain or past it all. I was sure of that.

When we drew closer we could hear shouts and laughter and a high keening wail. Despite these dismal sounds we scouted toward the house slowly.

On my left was Holt, a dark, capable comrade, and to my right my near brother, as reliable a fighter as ever was spawned by a terrible era, and the sensation of being with them on the prod was one of pride and remorseless energy. It felt like an old habit come back, and it was welcome.

Here I fit in—nay, I was necessary.

Before we quite reached the house we heard the hooves of the villains beating off. Thus encouraged, we sped up.

The burning house lit the scene too well. The bottom rooms billowed with flames and choking smoke rolled out. Evans lay in the yard, peaceful of pose but ripped of body. The mother stood over him, her face to the house, gleams in her spectacles. Honeybee clung to her skirts, a hysterical waif.

His bad expectations had proved correct for Evans. He was gone over the river, bless his soul.

"Oh, boys!" the mother howled. "They killed him, killed him, killed him!"

"How many are there?" Jack Bull asked.

"He is dead! What will I do? What will I do?"

I heard a rider on the road and thought it might be a straggler, so I went out to meet it. It was George Clyde, all out of breath.

"I heard the fracas," he said. "I thought you boys might be in a spot."

His coming cheered me. No odds buckled him down.

"How many?" Jack Bull shouted.

"Oh! Oh!" the new widow went. "A dozen or less. Vermin all."

"Well, shit, let's get them," Clyde said, and on down the road we went.

I checked my pistols as Old Fog's heart thumped between my legs. I had four loaded and ready. Our several pistols, and the many shots they afforded us over rifles, was the ace that allowed us to gamble with much larger groups. Close in we were mean with them, and many good things had come of that.

All kinds of fear and pride welled in me. If the mother had said they numbered forty, I believe we would still have given them chase. I was awful and my comrades were worse, but at times like these we made a wonderful company.

Down the dirt we pounded, hooves rumbling, no secrecy to cloak us at all. It did not matter if they heard us, for a fight was what we sought. This must always be admitted of us—for desperate dash and cruelty we were unbettered men.

The night had no shimmery glow to it, only darkness. Little could be seen. The ground was hard and the horses labored to keep the pace. Trees loomed over the lane and swaying spectral shadows lurched my heart.

Even foul villains have some sense. They waited on us and suddenly the night lit up as rifles banged away. We were as invisible to them as they were to us. The rounds whizzed ominously and we fired back at the flashes. After the first volley they rode in to mix, and the fight took place at huggy distances. This was a mistake.

"Traitors!" shouted a citizen vermin. "Kill the traitors!"

All the mortal frolic had mounts rearing and screaming, and Old Fog was caught up in the mood. He pranced and bucked. I fired as best I could.

One fellow was directly in front of me, so near I could smell his dinner, and I know I rid his horse of some hideous weight. He fell and I pegged him where he landed.

"Aw, hell," he whined, yellowed by my diligence.

A swung rifle splatted my knee.

It hurt.

Shouts and cries resounded. I shot and shot and willed myself into a smallish target. I believed I could not be hit, so absent had I decided myself to be.

The lane was now redone, made up with a couple of shot horses and maybe three villains.

Jack Bull Chiles was the nearest shadow to me. I knew the sound when he was hit. Even had he not cried out, I knew by the sound. His right arm flopped like a wet rag flung on a rail to dry. His pistol fell and his left hand slapped over the wound.

"You are hurt," I said.

He moaned.

Clyde, Holt and me chased the Federals a little ways, for they had tired of us quick. My knee already felt like a melon gone to mush. Luckily we did not chase far.

Jack Bull was hunched over. His breaths were fearsome deep things and he shook.

Clyde was in a state. He had dismounted and was pumping more lead into the dropped. Holt was still on horseback, jerking around, looking for something that he did not see.

"Jack Bull is hurt," I said. "I've got to get him home."

I grabbed the reins of Jack Bull's horse and turned about, leading my near brother to the dugout.

His moans and cries accompanied me.

When I dragged him into the dugout Sue Lee was there and screamed. My mushed leg straggled behind me, and there was windblown blood all over.

"Not this!" Sue Lee wailed. "Lord, *please* not this!"

In the light he looked bad. His arm was burst at the elbow, and cracked bone and torn meat and blood all showed. His eyes had crawled back in his head, leaving only the fluttering whites visible.

"He'll make it," I said. I was borrowing confidence on credit from faith. It wasn't really an attitude I had much of. But I needed it now, so I got it where I could. "I've seen worse-shot men do handsprings in a month."

The truth was his armbone was in shambles and a big bite of meat had been took—he was all shot to hell.

I set a pan of water on the fire. I took my big knife out and rested the blade on coals.

Sue Lee had grabbed her panic by the neck and choked it down to sensible action. She tied his arm above the wound to stifle the flow of blood.

My knee ached and swoll up so I could not bend the leg. It is a bad thing to have limbs that don't mind. Try as I might, I could not make the thing do right. Old friend agony was back with me.

In not too long a time George Clyde and Holt returned. They stamped in, looking grim and anxious. Clyde checked on Jack Bull and his first words were, "That fire has got to go out."

"I'm heating water," I said.

"Heat it quick. They'll come back with more men if they got them. We can't have a fire."

"He is bad," I said, nodding at Jack Bull.

"I see that. We'll have to take that arm off."

This horrified me.

"No!" I said. "We can heal it. He'll need it."

Clyde shook his head at me.

"Dutchy, we got no medical items or doctor sense amongst the whole group of us." He began to pace. "I can't go shanghai us a sawbones, neither. Federals are likely to be on us by sunup."

"We'll care for him," Sue Lee said. There was a sheet of ice over her eyes and her lips flinched as she spoke. I think she was starting to believe she was a jinx to her beau. "I can nurse him with Jake."

"As you say," Clyde said. "But you watch out green rot don't get started on him. Once it does it's over."

Holt sat near Jack Bull and watched him closely.

"It looks not too good, Jake," he said.

"God damn it! Don't nobody say that again." I had about heard all the bad news I could tolerate. You look at a bad thing and say it's bad so you know it's bad, then you forget it and go on. That's the only way.

12

WELL, SUE LEE and me together were about as good a doctor as a blind drunk moron from Egypt would be. I felt we came up shy of the mark. We washed his mangled right arm, then I took the red hot knife and burned the ragged wound closed. He screamed and jacked up and Holt shoved him down and the smell don't bear discussion.

Rough medicine was all I knew. I hoped it would work. Hope, I was learning, is a hardy comrade but not too trustworthy. It wouldn't do to count on him.

The dugout was black. Clyde had snuffed the fire and Holt was posted outside keeping watch. George could actually go to sleep, so he did. Sue Lee and me sat over my near brother, listening to him moan lowly, ready to smother his sounds if Federals came close.

I felt sick. My leg was a throbbing lame extremity. The idea that I might be crippled came and went. It seemed a selfish concern compared to Jack Bull's condition. He could die.

That point came home to me. To die had always been the trump card of fate, but it hadn't seemed likely to be played. Now, with him on the dirt, curled in pain, shattered of bone and minus some decent meat, it really did.

Finally Sue Lee fell asleep, one arm across Jack Bull's body. That left me alone and awake, listening tightly for the next wrong event to come stalking along in squadrons.

Long before new light hit, the dugout was cold. I covered the widow and the wounded, and shivered in my boots, observing the way my very breath wisped away from me. It seemed my whole life was jammed up and coughing globs, and this choking soul of mine had to be spit out in awful little spittles.

You can't rest that way.

I never did.

The world broke new again, and day sounds replaced the black quiet. The dugout was horrid with expectations. Only Clyde was rested well, and Federals and death seemed so likely that I just sat where I was, weak and sleepy, so scared I barely moved.

Jack Bull was washed down in color. His breaths bellowed and his eyes rolled around in his head. In daylight the wound was ugly and the signs of idiot doctoring looked just as bad.

Holt came in and said, "They is men on the road."

"How many?" Clyde asked. George went about his daily habits almost as usual.

"Several. But they ain't come into the woods."

"Keep a watch. I want to fight away from here if we got to fight."

Red had gotten into Sue Lee's eyes. She was wan and forlorn. The girl had pluck, but she was being sorely tested. How much bad she could take I did not know, but I hoped it was an awful lot, for that seemed to be her portion. The wound kept her busy. She washed at it, then rubbed grease over the rip.

Sometimes she raised his good hand and kissed the fingers. Her hair fell across her face and she whipped it back, then lifted his palm and licked it.

Her deeds often clashed with her face, for they seemed too sweet to be matched with her wild pretty look.

"What came of Mrs. Evans and Honeybee?" I asked. It had not occurred to me before. That made me blink with shame at the narrow field of my concern.

"The Willards took them up," Clyde said. "I reckon they will all be heading out of here by now."

"The Willards, too?"

"Oh, yes. They are ready to go south, clear roads or not. The idea that they could be next was hanging heavy on them."

We could not have a fire. It was clammy in the ground. I stared at Jack Bull's arm every little bit, studying it from all the angles as if I might understand what I saw. What could I do? I was ignorant but I knew it, so I would not play the fool by applying medicines of my own invention just to appear smart.

I reckon I looked wounded, too, dragging my sluggish leg about. Sue Lee sat next to me and whispered, "He is bad, but how are *you* feeling?"

Her concern startled me. I did not reply.

"Your leg," she said. "It must hurt."

"Oh, it does," I answered. "I've been here before, though."

"Can I help it?" she asked. There were dirt streaks on her cheeks, and her skin had bleached to a noble shade of pale.

"No." I patted her arm. "Try to rest yourself."

Her head shook and she grinned tightly.

"I doubt that," she said.

As time passed I thought of many things. Old Evans had went to Heaven instead of Texas, and a childish notion came to me: I wondered if we could bury him. It was out of the question, but I thought of it still. Such a Christian act might have soothed me, but they are so hard to perform when you are surrounded by circumstances.

The Federals did not come. This surprised me. They had to know we were somewhere in the neighborhood. Perhaps they figured we had fled. A pleasant thought would have been to think they found us so fierce they would rather avoid us, but I knew it was not true. About the same amount of courage was in them as in us, and there is no use in tall-talking to the contrary.

But this day was not to be our last, for whatever reason. As is the way with days, this one passed. Night fell. We lit a small candle. The dugout went from twilight chill to midnight cold. Jack Bull was buffeted about by agony, and fever gripped his person and made him do rambling talk. Most of his utterances were predictable — moans and so forth — but a few whole sentences splattered out of him.

"Do you hear the fish?" he asked of no one this side of Eternity.

I could hardly stomach it. He was bad off, and any improvement was days away.

George Clyde said, "Maybe I should try to get us a doctor."

"Where from?" I asked.

"There is one in Kingsville."

"That is fifteen miles. You can't cover it in one night."

"I know that, Dutchy." Clyde just wanted to be doing something. His energy was immense. "But I could lay up near there, then try to drag him back the next night."

"He may not want to come."

"Oh, I reckon he'll come. I have a special way of asking that works real good."

"Ah," I said, and nodded. "That might do."

We sat in the gloom and pondered this proposed venture. I didn't believe it could work. There were guns in Kingsville, and Missouri doctors were not new to this sort of situation.

"Will you take Holt?"

"No," Clyde answered. "Less men, less noise. Besides, if I can't get the doc, I'm heading on to Captain Perdee's. Holt'll help you and the widow."

"I wish you luck," I said.

In not much longer than it takes to tell it, he was gone. He rode off through the timber toward Kingsville, maybe to shanghai some mercy.

As he left, hope was with me, but I was getting suspicious of it, and did not toss a big embrace around it.

None of us were finicky eaters but dirt did not set with us, so we ate potatoes. There was no fire to bake them in or boil them over, so we ate them raw like apples and dreamed they were peaches.

Jack Bull Chiles could not chew. By the morning light I assessed his weakness. It was all he was was weak. The wound needed to be dressed and flushed by hot water, but there was none.

He had to eat.

"Sue Lee," I said. "We have got to feed him."

"I know, I know," she said. She was a run-down female. "But how?"

"The only way there is. Holt, toss me a tater."

When he tossed it, I caught it. I began to chew on the small dry thing, mashing my jaw over and over 'til I spit out a kind of white pap into my hand.

"Hold his head up," I said.

Sue Lee and Holt squatted at Jack Bull's side and raised his head. His lips were cracked and big black half moons were beneath his eyes. With two fingers I scooped the pap and stuck it in his mouth. He sputtered but swallowed, so I did it again. Little slobbers lit on his chin. I kept up the scoop-and-swallow work as long as he would take it. It was not for long. Hunger was not his main sensation.

We left him to rest as much as he would. Weird words were mumbled by him and nowhere in the dugout could you hide from them. They found you.

I went outside. There was no special thing to see. The wind smelled clean. The whole world was off from there, beyond the trees and sight.

The dugout plank creaked and out came Holt. He joined me on the dirt. He patted my back. He took slow breaths.

"I wonder," he said, "did you ever watch the rabbit? That is a pretty thing up close. Big eyes and a face that has changes in it, feelings like. It's got big fancy ears and is just a pretty thing but I still eat it. And it comes to me that I eat the pretty thing 'cause I am hungry."

"You tell interesting tales, Holt."

"Well, that's all of it." He touched my shoulder. "Jake, that arm is done for."

"Oh, I know it," I said. It was true. "I hoped it wouldn't be."

"It is done for."

"Maybe George will bring the doctor. He may see something we don't."

"Naw," Holt said. "I reckon he'll see what we see."

Possibilities ganged up on me. I felt clabbered by guilt, for only my dainty hopes had kept that arm from being took away sooner. Now Jack Bull was even weaker.

"Not now," I said. "We'll give George a chance first."

"The longer you wait," Holt said softly, "the harder it gets on the man."

"Oh, hellfire, will you just shut up on that? God damn it all, Holt, just give me peace for a while."

He laughed a rough one.

"Why not the moon?" he asked.

More pap was scooped as the day passed. I hoped to raise his strength. Sue Lee timed it out and we fed him regular as a babe.

Me and Holt switched off on keeping Federal watch. I thought of Texas and wished we were there and not any of us shot. If only wishing made it so, cripples would dance wild reels on tabletops and lots of good times would be had.

With no preamble at all Jack Bull began to speak.

"Jake," he said. "You look sad."

I went bug-eyed at him. He was awake and aware.

"We're taking care of you," I said, and scrambled to his side. "You can be mended."

"Don't lie, Jake. Don't lie to me. I can see. I can see to my own arm."

His fine American face was leeched dry of all emotion and interests save the drive to survive. The breaths he took were short and slow, as though fast deep ones would be beyond his control.

"George Clyde has gone for a doctor," I said.

Jack Bull nodded wearily, then said, "I always knew we would be killed. One or both of us."

"Well, that chance has always been there."

"Do you recall the pies on Mother's sill?"

"Of course. Those were good eating times."

"That they were." His big brown sick eyes went steady on me. "I always thought it'd be you, Jake. You dying. I was certain I would have to bury you."

This revelation tantalized me.

"I wish you were burying me," I said, but I knew I lied. It was strange how that hit me, too. I lied to my near brother, but I knew I lied and that freed me loose of some old notions I had fancied.

I didn't want to die in anyone else's place at all.

"Me, too," he said. His good hand clutched toward me and patted my knee. This was to tell me he joked, I think.

"You ain't dead, Jack Bull."

A slack spell came over him and his lips hung limp and he closed his eyes.

Our chat had roused Sue Lee and she came over and said,

"I'm right here." His eyes opened and he said, "Oh, good. Oh, good."

An instant later he went back to the gone state he had generally been in. His recess from delirium had been brief.

His veins became black. The black blood inched up the inside of his arm. Holt pointed it out first, then we all crouched over the arm and watched it somberly.

"We'll keep an eye on that," I said. "It can't be let go much longer." I looked at the widow and she was just about destroyed by knowledge. "I might have to take it off as best I can."

We sat around then, waiting for blackened veins of wronged blood to force me to surgery. The waiting was a chore. I felt my mushed knee to amuse myself. I squeezed the kneecap and nothing wiggled or stuck up sharply. It was only a terrific bruise.

"I wonder how Honeybee is," Sue Lee said. She spoke dreamily. "That is a sweet little girl. Her elbows jiggle still. Maybe she is a little fat, but that Honeybee is sure enough sweet."

"Don't I know it," I said. "Her voice does pleasantries to any song she tackles."

"Oh, my, yes," the widow said, almost brightly. "That child reads better than I ever will, too."

An awesome responsible streak was in Holt. I saw him check on Jack Bull, then he said, "Now. It has got to be done now. The black streaks is pushing up to the armpit."

Sue Lee grabbed my hand, her big whipped eyes practically speared into me.

"Can you do it, Jake? Can you do it for him?"

I nodded and thought about what must be done. My belly jammed with nettles. My head felt loose from me. I went outside. The sun was gone. It was cold, cold, cold, and I knelt on the frozen ground and it all came up. It just all jumped up out of me and slopped to the dirt. I retched and retched and thought I never would quit—I had to cut him!

"Don't think about it, Roedel," Holt said from behind me. "Just do it. There ain't no sliding around it. Just you do it or else I will."

"Oh no you won't," I said. "His family raised me. I reckon it'll be me who saws his rotten arm off."

Back in the dugout I did things, but it was like it wasn't the true me. My hands were busy and half smart and lashed a rope above the spot where I would cut and readied the blade.

"If he screams too loud we may all die," I said. "Put a stick in his mouth. Don't let him scream too loud."

Holt put the bit in.

"Sue Lee," I said, "sit on his chest and keep his jaws clamped on that stick. Holt, you shove him down wherever he starts to flop."

I ran my fingers across Jack Bull's face, and the skin had the feel of cabbage. I owed him so much. The whole life I had. I studied the arm and the fouled veins and laid the blade at the spot. Then, nerved up to the highest pitch I could summon, I began to saw.

The job was miserable.

I was no good.

Sue Lee held on tight to his jaw and Holt held him down and I held the blade and everyone made noises.

Oh, sweet Lord Jesus.

It was way down there past terrible.

13

HE KNOT ON the rope was not enough of a bind, and loosened to leak Jack Bull Chiles. My world bled to death. I couldn't get the cut burned closed. It was too moist. The smell was a horrible fact.

I guess I wept. I guess we all wept. Even Holt wept. It's a useless reaction. No comfort at all.

We sat there all night. The wind made sad, tormenting sounds. Once, Sue Lee put her fingers to her hair, grabbed a hold and beat her head around like she was churning butter. She shrieked and I listened. I had nothing for her.

Words can't match it.

Past a certain point I could not sit. I picked up the shovel and contemplated a grave. I wanted it to be inside the dugout where he had lived, not off in coyote-prowled timber. I measured a spot in the center of the dugout. There wasn't much light, but I didn't need much. I vented some bad feelings on the soft dirt. The shovel slammed down in my hands, gouging out little loads of dirt, which I flung to the corners. The clods pattered down like varmint feet scurrying over leaves. I beat a hole right into the ground, flinging dirt in the dark.

Sweat broke out on me. I relished the evidence of effort. I hung my tongue down and lapped the salty beads as they fell from my nose.

This was all there was to do.

The sun ignored our grief and kept to its routine. The lightened scene was harrowing. Sue Lee appeared awful and used up. Holt was far gone into pious reflection.

I gestured at the grave.

"Bury him," I said. "Quick."

For lack of alternatives, leadership fell on me. Holt and the widow began to roll Jack Bull toward the grave, spinning him across the dusty floor.

We dropped him down and threw his arm in after him. For some reason I kicked my satchel of mail into the pit alongside him. I think I was guilty about my luck. Then I eased a shovelful of dirt onto his chest.

"Wait!" Sue Lee said. "Wait a minute, Jake. I want to look at him."

She knelt next to the grave, leaned over and kissed Jack Bull's blue lips.

This act of hers moved me. I went into prayer position at her side. Many things hidden in me were being hinted out, and I stared down at Jack Bull Chiles and dredged up all the farewell feelings I had. I bent over. I did something to him dead I had never tried on him alive. I kissed him good-bye, right where she had, just the same.

Holt humphed behind me. I looked up at him, and he watched me oddly.

"Did you see something that bothers you, Holt?"

His face was smooth, and he shook his head briskly.

"No, no," he said and turned away. "I didn't see it."

I finished the funeral. The grave made a mound. No good verses came to mind, so it was a stoic ceremony.

"So long," I said. "See you over the river."

Outside it was gray. A late March storm was coming in from the north. The clouds looked soiled and the light was dull.

"Let's get to Captain Perdee's," I said. "We'll rally with the boys. It's time to start the war back up."

I claimed two of Jack Bull's four pistols and gave the others to Holt. We hung them from our saddles and put the widow on top of Jack Bull's horse.

I wanted to be moving and never in that dugout again.

"Keep an eye out for George," I said.

"I am," Holt answered. "But I bet he at Perdee's."

We kept to the timber. The day got colder, then it pitched snow at us. The wind shoved the flakes into our faces but we hunched over and rode on. By midday Sue Lee had surrendered to fatigue. Holt and me took a rope and tied her into the saddle. She uttered neither complaints nor praise. She was past that.

The horses sent plumes of breath from their nostrils and slogged through the snow. Some inches of the white stuff had gathered on the ground. The wind blew our tracks away as quick as we made them. No Federals crossed our path. If you weren't desperate, you wouldn't be out in such weather. I steered us toward Captain Perdee's, where I hoped we would find plenty of comrades. Sue Lee would be sent to some safer southern haven. Me and Holt would fight another season. The deeds of winter demanded it.

I kept us rolling beyond nightfall, and the snow kept blowing and nothing much could be seen. We lumbered along blindly in the woods and did not speak.

Around midnight we came upon a burned house. Some weak citizen had lost all here. Two walls still stood and we took cover, huddling next to them.

I wrapped Sue Lee's blanket around her and she slept. My body bid me join her. She shivered in sleep, so I spread my blanket over us both and lay against her. This warmed us but, tired as I was, I could not sleep.

So I listened to her breathe. The girl was good as double widowed and only seventeen. She'd seen a mirror of hell, I guess. Her breaths had a ragged rhythm. A bad sleep cadence. But her body was warm.

It was good to know her.

Curling up to her was a saving human exercise, as it reminded me that I lived, and diverted me from recollections of all I had lost, which was all there was.

BOOK THREE

Many cry in trouble and are not heard, but to their salvation.

— ST. AUGUSTINE

14

ALL THAT YEAR we were dying. The hairbreadth instinct some call luck had slowed on us. They killed us in groups and pairs and alone. We fell in timber, haylofts, fighting on the field and lying wounded helpless in borrowed beds.

Oh, we hit back.

Within sight of Kansas City twenty-eight Federals hauling grain made our acquaintance. They knew we rode under the Black Flag, so they fought to the end. Our reputation for thoroughness gave the Federals a kind of forlorn ferocity. "They know prisoners are not our style," George Clyde said. This was true wherever we fought, and it was true of us when the upper hand was theirs.

When we all rallied at Captain Perdee's in late March it was clear by the jumpy look in previously calm faces, the despondent gaze in unblinking eyes, that our struggle had carried us into a new territory of the soul, where we found new versions of our selves.

Cave Wyatt, Riley Crawford, the Hudspeths, Turner Rawls and Black John welcomed us all. There was much backslapping and sharing of tales, which led to sadness or guffaws. Several southern men would ride with us no more, but we didn't dwell on that.

Sue Lee Shelley was not the only female refugee in camp. The Federals had gotten in the habit of arresting our women, so we had a gaggle of wives and sisters and sweethearts in our midst. We convoyed them to the Perche Hills and left them there among the hidden patriots of that district.

By summer the most common comments were those that roughly compared Lawrence, Kansas, to Hades. The Jayhawkers operated from that place and operated meanly. Few lives in western Missouri went untouched by their depradations.

"Lawrence must be reduced to rubble," Black John said. Various echoes of this sentiment were heard, and we began to ponder a visit there.

In July, a hot terrible month, me, Holt, Riley Crawford and Turner Rawls were riding near Bone Hill, scouting for a Unionist who called himself Major Grubbs. The citizens thereabouts had complained of him and his boastful treacheries, so we set off to counsel him toward a more humble attitude.

"I want to kill him," Riley said. Riley's boyish face held eyes as hard as any demon's. The boy had been weaned from hope, and only bloodshed raised his morale. "I want to kill them all. Anymore that's all I think about."

We followed a slight creek, our mounts splashing in the shallows. Whiskey was in it with us. Lately it was always in us. It made the world seem slower, more possible to defeat. This was a necessary delusion.

Within sight of Bone Hill, a clapboard village, we accosted a farmer driving hogs down a lane with a stick and two dogs. He was nervous in our presence and got more so when Turner put a pistol at his head and demanded, "Whar dis Mador Groobs?"

"What?" the farmer said. The hogs grunted off and about with the dogs yapping after them. "What did you say?"

"Where does Major Grubbs stay?" I asked.

"Oh," the farmer said. I could see the tendency toward slyness in the skittering of his eyes. "You boys don't want him. He's a dangerous fellow. You just leave him be."

Turner, who knew his own mind, shot the farmer in the foot.

"Sown bits!" he shouted. "Whar dis Groobs?"

"Over east!" the farmer howled. He landed on his butt and held his boot full of rearranged toes. "He stays at the Dorris place! It's on a hill with apple trees, God damn you." There was true fright in him now. "You boys didn't need to shoot me."

"Shut your damned mouth," I told him. "And don't you go raise the alarm or we'll find you and roast your mother in front of you."

On down the lane we went, sharing the rotgut, woozily certain of victory. The lane led us up a small rise and past a rock wall that ran in front of a charred house. We were noisy. Turner had fired a shot. We were two steps into drunk.

At the rock wall they opened up on us. Even drunk I understood that we had blundered, and wheeled Old Fog about, swinging loosely in the saddle. There were twenty or more of them, all mounted and miserable, and it seemed to me they gloated.

"Oh, shit!" I said. "It's Jayhawkers!"

No debate was required over our course of action—we fled.

They chased. Bullets zinged by or chimed off rock or plumed blood from a horse's ass. We shot back while fleeing, an exercise we had gotten pretty good at.

The retreat took us back to the farmer and the hogs and the dogs. He was doing a hobbled variant of the sprint, and I guessed he had known Jayhawkers were in the area. Holt sized things the same and called the farmer a son of a bitch, then shot him down right in the midst of the squealing hogs and yapping dogs.

"Kill the secesh!" the Jayhawkers shouted. Their attitude was one of mean confidence, and they had a right to it. They loved murdering us in small, safe clusters.

We hadn't got far when Riley caught one in the soft area below the ribs. It went from back to front. The ball split that loose flesh wide. It made an instant mess of him, but he clung to the saddle horn.

Holt and me spun around and took aim. This caused them to pull up a bit, and we blasted away at them, hoping only to stall them long enough for Riley to clear out. But they were too many, so we rejoined the flight.

They thundered after us, saying terrible things and winging shots at us. Old Fog was creased in the haunches and bolted ahead in a horsey panic. Down to the south, beyond a long meadow, the timber was thick.

"Get to timber," Holt said, saucer-eyed. "Get to timber."

Hell, we took off that way, but the Jayhawkers hung tough and little Riley had his hands full. We couldn't pull ahead of them. At the timberline Turner and Holt and me faced them and displayed enough good aim to send them down the meadow, where they could enter the timber and hunt us.

"I can't ride," Riley said. Wrong parts of him hung over his belt. He wasn't even sixteen and he was ruined. "Put me down, please. Please. Please, put me down."

Dark wasn't coming on fast enough to help us. We had to keep running. That is one thing bushwhackers know. The thick green leaves shielded us for the moment, but right away we could hear the Jayhawkers trotting into the timber a short distance away.

"Please, please," went Riley.

I stepped down and pulled the ripped-wide boy off his mount and set him against a tree. He held his hands where he was spilling, and that pale thing that happens to the mortally wounded was happening to him.

"Leave me my guns," he said. "Don't take 'em. Leave 'em." Riley was a kid like no kid I ever knew. "I might get one."

I cocked a pistol and laid it near him. Turner was grunting some fierce riddle and Holt was prancing about. We had to go.

"Riley," I said. I put my palm to his face and squeezed his cheek. "You got to fire at them, Riley. Bring them down on you."

"I will, Jake. Boys, I will." He was crying, and rippling with pain. "I was a good boy, wasn't I?"

"As good as they come," I said, and remounted.

We took off. I looked back once and saw Riley hunched to the tree, his face to the sky.

A sneak through the woods was our plan. It is a hard trick to bring off on horseback. Noise was made. The Jayhawkers were shouting commands to fan out and flush us. Pretty quick after that Riley's shots sounded. That was our notice to lay on the spurs and we did it.

In a minute there were more shots, then silence.

"Tough boy," Holt said. "But he didn't hold them long."

Even as he spoke I heard hooves beating the earth, branches cracking and dangerous voices. We were in a low spot, thick with bramble, that ran between two rises. A gully twisted down toward the south.

"Follow this gully," I said. "If we got to, we'll break their line."

Turner led. Flinches had come to roost on his face, and the whole gamut of his features bobbled. Holt took up the rear, and in the undertones of his breath I believe I caught a snatch of a hymn.

Before we'd gone two hundred feet I saw two men on the rise to the east. I hoped to kill them before they saw us, and then they did see us, and I think they had had the same idea in store for us, so both opinions were disappointed.

Everybody looked for a tree to hide behind.

"Oh, Lor'!" Turner cried. "Dey's god us."

"We'll break through," I said. All the horses were jittery and jerking around, but fighting on foot was for morons. "Let's do it now. Attack those two now, it's our only chance."

Fright may have been our regular pastime, but hesitancy was not a bushwhacker trait. We tore right into them, and they plowed downhill to meet us. Clean shots were hard because of the trees, and bark flew hither and yon, and we trilled rebel yells for all we were worth, and you had better believe that we could raise a cry that would have you filling your boots.

When we closed on them, between two spacious, fat oaks, the shots were so rapid as to be mesmerizing. One of the Jay-hawkers had a red feather in his hat and a rotten face. He aimed on Holt but I got him. I busted him open at the neck and the teat and he fell a corpse.

His comrade lost heart on seeing this and retreated, call-ing wildly for help.

We then did a tactical move that consisted entirely of run-ning away.

After a quarter mile of panicked scrambling, we came to a clearing and just about flew across it. I looked over my shoul-ders and, oh, shit, yes, there they were, coming on after us.

The horses we rode were as fine a breed of beasts as there has ever been. They had bottom and sand and some vague beasty knowledge that we required all of it right then. We ran them hard all afternoon, and the Jayhawkers fell back but stayed in sight until dark.

In the night we made a big loop to the south, then swung west, west to our comrades.

That day had been too near a thing.

15

A LL THAT SEASON they were driven to us. Woeful widows with hung husbands and squalling babes. White-haired grannies with toothless mouths and fierce feelings. Hard-faced farm boys who would now apprentice themselves to the study of revenge.

They had been run from their homes, burned out, turned out, and set adrift to die. Western Missouri had a pitiful legion of raggedy citizens.

"Look at them," Cave Wyatt said. "The damned Yankees will starve the children to sadden the fighters. It is a mean game."

And it was, and we were its counterpart.

It was in that same terrible month of July that the Federals arrested Black John's sisters. They were imprisoned in the upstairs of a liquor supply house at Kansas City.

Black John became frantic to exact a price for this breach of the rules. He ranted and preached blue peril, and threatened to do wonders to entire armies.

One morning I watched Black John holding a hand mirror while combing his hair. He peered at his reflection and said,

"How do you do, Black John?" Then smiled, and answered himself, "Damned fine, Mr. Ambrose, damned fine."

For a while we went back to wearing Yankee blue uniforms. They were easy to come by. The trick of it was so simple, but it worked peachy. Twenty or thirty of us would ride up to a scout of Federals and George Clyde would say, "How is rebel hunting today, lieutenant?" and before an answer could be uttered or suspicions raised on closer inspection, we would cut open on them point-blank and pass them through to the next world. The treachery of it was not too noble, but it was a rare day when it failed.

I had not seen Sue Lee for a few months. I knew she had gone to Henry County and was living with the kin of Howard Sayles. I thought often of her but had little news until Howard approached me in camp and said, "That Sue Lee gal is with child, Roedel."

His expression was somewhat stern.

"She is?" I said. "I didn't know it."

"Well, now you do, damn it." Howard spit and glowered at me. "You better go marry her, boy. It ain't right not to."

"Me?" I said. "No, not me. I don't got to marry nobody."

"Is that right?" Howard Sayles was thirty or even older, and the youthful manners of his comrades often served to annoy him. "You're that kind of man, eh, Dutchy?"

I reckon my face sterned up some, too, and I said, "I will take care of her, Sayles. And you have said about all the rough things to me you had better."

This man smirked at me.

"Is she your woman of light love, Dutchy? 'Cause we don't want the scandal of it on our names down home. That gal needs a husband and quick."

"It'll be took care of somehow," I said. "When it can be."

He softened upon hearing that.

"That's all I ask," he said. "I know now ain't the right time. Hell, we all do things." He gave me a playful punch on the shoulder. "Everybody likes her real good, you know. I don't want you to believe otherwise."

"I never did."

Later that night I told Holt of Sue Lee's predicament. He pursed his plump lips, and gazed down, weighted by heavy thought.

"Could be you ought to," he said finally. "I've thunk it from several sides, and could be she'd make you a fine wife."

"But there is one thing we ain't mentioning here," I said. "It might be she don't *want* to marry me. That is, even if I did want to marry *her,* she might not."

I could not tell whether he thought me a pessimist or a lame-brain, but it was plain he figured I was something slow.

"Now, how could that be?" he asked.

At this time George Clyde ambled over, hauling a tin of beans, and stood near us. He had a curious attitude on his face.

"You two sure got to be pals, didn't you?" he said. He looked at both of us, and I wondered if he had come to feel like the spare wheel. "Ever since winter you two boys have been clapping your gums together regular as crones."

I told him about Sue Lee. He laughed and said, "Hell, that's Chiles's baby she's lugging. I think so, anyhow."

I just looked at him sourly.

"Don't tell me it's yours even if it is," he said.

"It ain't."

"Then don't be a lunkhead, Dutchy. Marry some girl who is pregnant from you—that's the fun part, anyhow."

"If you say it is, then I reckon it is," I said. "I don't rightly know. But maybe I ain't ripe for marrying up with nobody. Maybe it's the bachelor way for me."

"Ah," went Clyde. He bobbed his chin in approval. "That's even more fun, Dutchy. You are showing some sense."

He said I was, and I supposed it could be true, but I wondered what opinion I might shift to if I was looking at her sweet busted tooth, or that fascinating scar down her brow, or those hot dark eyes.

The Federals kept us moving. Large bodies of bluebellies would ride into our area and we would scatter to rendezvous at a choicer spot. Often a few hands would not show up who should have and we would figure them dead.

In this manner we saw a good portion of Missouri. Whole neighborhoods of ash and splintered glass awaited us. Chimneys stuck up alone, the one thing left solid by the whirl of destruction. The roads were clogged by refugees who'd been robbed of everything but the garb they wore.

It just let the grease right out of your heart to see them.

Where the chance of it was fair, we chastised the enemy. They were so many, though, and we so few. I believe that by late summer we all felt we were being whipped. This did not turn us meek, but it numbed our spirits a grade or two.

So many of us died rudely.

Near Austin, in Cass County, after a draining ride on a skillet-hot day, we rode up on two old women in grimed attire. The old gals were headed for Texas and not going to make it from the looks of them. They glanced over us, then one of them said to the other, "Rebels, Isis. These men are rebels."

"So I see," said the other granny. "When it's too late for them to help, they rush up spoilin' for a fight."

Black John nodded down at the women and showed some irritation at their sarcasm.

"Show us Yankees, ladies, and we will hurt them."

The old gals looked glum. One of them pointed off down a lane that ran east and said, "Go on thataway 'til you see a burned barn, mister bushwhacker. You go on down past the barn and into the tree line, why don't you? You'll find an interestin' thing there."

"What might that be?" Black John asked.

"Oh, rebels. Some of the rebels are hanging around up in there."

We followed their directions and rode right under their granny pun. High in the branches, seasoned beyond recognition, there swung seven noosed rebels. It was macabre and altogether eerie. The bodies draped down through the leaves like rancid baubles in the locks of a horrible harlot.

"I bet it's Carter McPhee," Cave Wyatt said. Cave pointed to high up in the great tree. "I bet it's Carter McPhee and I reckon some of those others are Raphael McPhee and the Price brothers. I can't be sure. They all rode with Quantrill."

Time allowed for it, so we did some Christian spade work. The Yankees hung men like this to taunt and torment local patriots. Such murders were inspirational to us. Any southern man or deluded Federal who was caught burying ex-rebels was shot by the soldiers. This habit led to many southern dead rotting for months in plain sight.

In this instance we set that straight, but I think all of us boys got a nervous preview of our own futures.

After a while, these things got to you. At times like this I was often feeling Jack Bull's dead hand on my shoulder. It was the heavy touch of grim memory. All it made me was forlorn, but it kept coming back. That is the way with grievous knowledge, you can never get far enough ahead of it.

What really ripped it was when the women's prison in Kansas City collapsed. The girls were mashed like rose petals in the family Bible. Unionists had weakened the walls by digging under the foundation, and this had got them what they wanted—the death of our womenfolk.

Two of Black John's three sisters were killed and the third was crippled. Five other true southern women perished as well, one of them Riley Crawford's mother and one of them Pitt Mackeson's wife.

Black John did not take it well. I did not take it well either. Bushwhackers and fence sitters and even some Federals took it badly. All along the border frothy anger and crazed plots of revenge began to be howled.

The Federals had crossed over the last line of restraint. And believe you me, we were the wrong tribe to treat in that fashion.

Riders came and went from all over the territory. Every little nest of bushwhackers was being called on to rally with Captain Quantrill on the Blackwater River. We went to the place, and so did the men of Thrailkill, Poole, Jarrett, Younger, Cobb and Todd.

It was a sullen and dangerous gathering. The boys of every group were outraged by the smashed women and the murders of comrades and the hopeless war.

Our group, a mix of Ambrose and Clyde men, was one of the larger gangs. Quantrill's was the largest, with about a hundred and twenty famous fighters, but some of the others were only family-sized bands.

Captain Quantrill had credentials of consequence all over the region and in many parts of the nation. He was a girlish man in appearance, with fine features and heavy-lidded eyes. He killed in bulk and at every opportunity. He was loved by many.

"Patriots of the South!" he shouted down to us from a wagon bed. "It is time we strike back! The Yankees believe they can drive our people from their homes and kill us with impunity. They have gotten the notion that so unmanly are we, so toothless a gang of masculine specimens, that they can kill our women as leisurely as if it were a sport. Well, it ain't so and we all know it. We're going to Lawrence, boys, and root the rats right out of their holes!"

The grisly audience raised hoorahs at this, for Lawrence was the place on the map we most wanted to blot off it. But I looked around me at the mingling bands of desperadoes and thought, Saying it is one thing, but pulling it off is another.

I went over to George Clyde, who was beaming with anticipation.

"George," I said. "Lawrence is forty-five miles into Kansas. There are whole armies out there and no friends at all."

"You got it, Dutchy," Clyde said jovially. "It'll be a shock-arooni of a surprise to the bastards. They sleep heavy out there, believing they are safe from us."

Well, I did not argue it with Clyde, but it turned out that many of the boys shared my thoughts. "We'll never make it back," Cave Wyatt said. "Even if we can get there, they'll chop us down on the prairies. But I reckon we'll give that town some memories first."

As I strolled about the camp, I heard many echoes of this sentiment. Almost no one planned on needing more gulps of air after this trip. There were scads of Federals out there, so we thought we were seeing Missouri for the last time.

It figured to be a bitter killing spree in the town, house-to-house fighting with all the Yanks out there, then it would end in a vigorous form of mass suicide once the armies caught up to us. This frame of mind was fueled by a flood of whiskey. Dumb and bold things are best accomplished drunk, we figured, so we went deep into the popskull.

The night before setting out we stayed drunk, rambunctious with anticipation, and thereby took a miss on sleep. I found myself sharing jugs with strangers who rode my side of the road, and got up-close glimpses of some of our ilk who had become famous. Frank James doddered around with Coleman Younger, and Kit Dalton staggered about with the Basham brothers and the Pence brothers and Payne Jones and Peyton Long. These men were all notorious above and beyond most of us, and waddled about the camp, blind drunk and not noticeably special.

Riding with such earnest men gave me confidence.

"Holt," I said, "this band will be the Spartans in a few histories someday."

Holt looked at me slack-lipped, flustered by rotgut, and said, "That so? I wouldn't know."

By dawn I was too whiskey-weary to care about much. Quantrill started us off for Lawrence early. There were over three hundred riders and the sight of us was awesome: long flowing southern hair beneath slouch hats; broken-in border shirts; a great harvest of pistols hanging everywhere; and fuzz-cheeked faces beneath busthead-reddened eyes.

I joined a scout party in the lead of the main group. George Clyde rode at the front, for he knew the wrinkles in that neighborhood, having been there before to tangle with Jim Lane's Kansans. His gaze went everywhere, looking quickly on this, then quicker on that, nodding his head at landmarks that had not shifted.

The sun was a merciless yellow presence. Heat lapped up from the baked dirt and the horses breathed rattly. The land was level pretty much and light on shade trees.

By noon we were south of Spring Hill, Kansas. Captain Quantrill called a halt. There were Federal posts within the next few miles, and his plan called for us to slip by them at night. So we fell out around a scummed-over pond and bore down on the whiskey 'til dark.

My mind had broken the leash, spurred on by fatigue and busthead, and dragged back thoughts I never wanted. A quality I didn't care for came out in me. I pitied myself. I pitied myself and my lot in life. That is a mangy introspection and not one I petted much. But there it was, a weak thought languishing between my ears. Life had been a big boohoo.

I wondered if I truly was diseased in the brain. Then I looked at my comrades: some of them were engaged in pegging stones at bullfrogs, while others oiled pistols or snuggled to the jug. This made me wonder the same thing, only louder.

Babe and Ray Hudspeth sat next to me for a spell. These boys were looking on the bright side. Babe said, "There's a store in Lawrence called Bush's Delicacies and Apparel, Dutchy. It's packed from floor to ceiling with fine clothes and smoked hams and sweet breads. We aim to rob it right off. Be with us, why don't you?"

"I might be."

"Good. You won't go wrong." Babe's glazed eyes rolled up and he laughed. "If we *do* make it home, we'll be rich with duds and meat."

"That's right," Ray said. He was slightly older than Babe but more reserved. "They can't count on gettin' every single one of us."

When the world was black enough to travel sneaky in, we

got going. We circled past the post at Spring Hill, and though I believe they noticed us, we encountered no challenges.

My eyes felt raw and it was hard to hold them open. Old Fog stepped deftly enough, but every jolt was a jolt. In the back of the pack drunks sang until hushed. Odd snatches of laughter drifted around. "I ain't hardly over gettin' shot near the jewels at Blue Cut," I heard someone say. "But I wouldn't miss this for six chicken wings." A man I didn't know tapped my shoulder and held a bottle toward me. "Take a bracer of Old Crow, partner," he said. "It won't keep the gnats from your eyes but it'll make 'em cuter to you." I tried his medicine and slid further into drunk than I wanted to be.

Lawrence would take all night getting to. By midnight we were lost. The leaders had a conference and decided to recruit guides. At the next house we saw, the man of it was dragged out and made to guide us as far as he could. When he, too, was lost, a big red-haired man named Pringle slit his throat and we got a new guide at the next house.

Before long I could barely stay in the saddle. I had Holt lash me in so if I went blank and fell I wouldn't break my neck. Many of the boys were roped in the same. It was hard traveling.

I dozed on horseback, awaking in flashes, witnessing scenes more garish than any I'd ever encountered. It was an odd state I was in and my senses were fragmented and my mind ricocheted off of what I did see or thought I saw.

The whole long trip was passing strange. My eyes opened to see a bald man on his knees beneath a torch, his tongue gripped by the driving hand of one of us. It did not keep me awake. "Yeah, that's right," a voice said softly. "I'm from Liberty, with Jarrett. I lived around Liberty 'til I couldn't no more." A hand shoved me and I started up to see Cave Wyatt. "Sweet dreams, Dutchy boy?" he asked. "You looked so peaceful I couldn't stand it." The rhythm of the horse's gait could be adjusted to. If you were ready to die, it didn't wake you. "Mother," I said in German, out loud or in a dream, "the dishes are in the yard where I tossed them. I won't do them. Jack Bull doesn't do them. I want to trap beaver in the mountains like Jim Bridger." Another torch scene halted my horse, and the end of movement awakened me. "Are you takin' us in circles, you Dutch bastard?" "No, no," the man cried. "I swear, I don't even know any circles." I saw him bludgeoned, and we went back on the move. I just couldn't avoid sleep. My eyelids were like weighted shades. Someone near me said, "Oh, don't mess with him, Jim. He's a Dutchman, but a good one. He's been with Black John a long while." Later, when it was I don't know, I was nudged awake by Holt. "Remember Jack Bull?" he asked. "Yes," I answered. "Me, too," he said, and rode on by me. I went back to where I had been, wondering if we'd actually spoken. The steps kept up. I recognized the voice of Black John as he passed up and down the line. "No survivors," he said. "The time for them is gone. I don't want any survivors old enough to cock a gun, boys. None." A very vivid fiction got done in my mind: I saw Alf Bowden blasting my father in the neck, then booting his old foreign butt along Main Street, blood spurting in a stream, kicking the old fellow past Asa Chiles and Jackson Evans. I saw me and Jack Bull seated on a blanket near a high stoked fire, playing faro with the Dutch boy I back-shot and several mashed sisters.

That got me conscious. I came awake and stayed there. I searched the ranks for Holt and gained his side. He was asleep. His head hung forward on his chest and he snored. I shook him and said, "Don't let them bother you, Holt. It's only dreams."

His head nodded slowly, then eased back to his chest.

A strange Quantrillian in a red shirt drew abreast of me. His head was shaking constantly. "Why couldn't they leave us be?" he asked. "They have their place, they didn't need to come roughshod into ours. Why didn't they just leave us be?"

I could give him no answer but a red-eyed stare, so he rode up to the next man and said, "Why didn't they just leave us be?"

16

CAPTAIN QUANTRILL HAD timed our march exquisitely. Just as the cocks commenced to crow we came in sight of the hated city. It was spread out before us, peaceful and asleep, as convenient as a one-table banquet.

"Form into fours," Quantrill commanded.

Mount Oread loomed on the far side of the town, and there, on the south pouty lip of the Kaw River, were the households of splendor, made so by our ransacked riches.

"Burn the town! Kill, kill, kill!"

Spurs dug into flanks and we came on, all as one, desperate and crazed, in terrible number, bent on revenge by bloody work, fully expecting to take on legions, and my emotions had the range of a rainbow. With my throat choked, clotted by fear and rage, my eyes sprang leaks, and I looked about me, trembling with some sort of occult joy, for we were men and unapologetic, dashing down the slope, pistols primed—oh, there was wonder in it!

I saw the first man fall, a doughty, salt-haired, surprised man, milking a cow, and he died right there beneath the teat.

Yip-yipping for all we were worth, we ravaged into the town. Men in long johns, sleepy still, were chased into their yards and pistoled down. I saw a whirl of men split off and ride into a camp of recruits near the center of town. They were yet in slumber inside their white tents, and we fired into their bedrolls and brought them crawling out. It was all niggers. Uniformed niggers raised extra frenzy in the boys, and the hectic potshotting and dodging went up a notch. I think two or three of the niggers made it to the brush bottoms of the river and escaped. I don't know. I thought they were an army, and I guess I got one.

By now the citizenry was coming awake and was scrambling or skulking after hiding places. Everywhere you turned, they were being shot. Voice was given to many agonized sensations. The women wailed. Children screamed.

There was no army in sight. The citizens never even fired a shot to defend themselves. A great many of them stood on the streets and looked on us dumbstruck, as if they couldn't believe we were just who we looked like we were.

Why didn't they hide? Why didn't they flee? Why on earth did they not fight us?

The women tried to shield their men; then, when that failed, to beg for mercy. It just wasn't going to come. This place was well hated, and had talked tough about us for years, and sent Jayhawkers all over us and ours. The day had come for us to give it back.

In the melee I found the Hudspeths at the delicacy shop they had mentioned, tying hams and greatcoats to their mounts. Other men had broken open the saloons, and pretty quick all of us were drunk again. Yankee flags were knotted on horse tails and dragged down the dirty streets. There was constant gunfire and pandemonium.

At the north end of town I saw about twenty white recruits mowed down in the sun. Their rifles weren't even loaded. They were not set up to fight. They never got their chance at us.

Pretty soon the place was in flames.

Quantrill, Black John and Clyde raced all over bellowing brutal strategy: "Burn 'em out, they'll come!"

I saw Holt at The Eldridge House, standing with Quantrill's nigger, an older man called Nolan. To me it seemed all of this drunken revenge might overfill the bucket and slop onto them. They understood that, I think. They weren't going anywhere.

The Eldridge House was for some reason special to Quantrill, so he didn't want it burned yet. I went up to Holt and Nolan.

"Let's us get some eggs," I said.

The two of them were sharing a bottle. Holt's eyes were bloody.

"Yeah, Jake. Let's get all the eggs they got and some ham."

We went inside. The owner and his wife were frantic trying to feed all the boys who were already in there. Customers of the hotel were lined up to a wall and were being robbed by Arch Clay, Turner Rawls, Payne Jones and some others. A pair of dead men were crumbled to the floor. Even ladies' handbags and wedding rings were taken.

"Give me some," I said, and took the bottle from Holt. A

long pull on it convinced me I really was there and it really was happening. I said, "I ain't hungry no more," and went outside.

I saw men flushed like rats from burning houses right into the harsh embrace of the end. I saw all the varieties of robbery there could possibly be getting done. I saw women shoved in the dirt of God's green earth, and little boys shot in the head.

Quite a number of the men were not joining in on the fray. They stood about looking shocked, stamping their feet, shaking their heads. This thing was out of hand.

I went and stood with them.

"They ought not to murder the children," a gray-haired rebel said.

"But pups make hounds," I said. I had to believe that.

"If it was your pup, you'd feel different, son."

These men were farmers turned fighters and not comfortable with the tableau of a massacre. And that was all this was, easy mayhem on a grand scale.

"For God's sake, where are their armies?" I said. "Why don't they come and fight?"

But they didn't do it. There were no legions of soldiers to be found and damned few Jayhawkers were at home. I had come here, as had these other rebels, for a desperate fight, but there wasn't one to be had. It was only bad-luck citizens finding out just how bad luck can be.

The gray-haired rebel next to me walked off, followed by a few of the other shocked southerners. I went with them. I don't know why.

We walked down the street, stepping around looters who were strapping all manner of plunder to their horses. Glass was shattered everywhere. Oaths were screamed, shots fired, blood let, and a din of loud insane laughter kept up.

At a hostelry a freckle-faced woman went to her knees and begged Pitt Mackeson not to kill her husband. I stared right into her face and she looked like every woman you'd ever known.

"I'll show him the same mercy they showed us," Mackeson said. He then put the husband through to the other side via a bullet in the ear.

Around a corner from the main street there were rows of houses. Several of us walked right into one and sat down. There was a wrinkled woman in there, a wrinkled man and a boy who was old enough. All of them were cowering.

"Feed us," the gray-haired reb said.

It fell on the woman to answer.

"Gladly, men," she said, about as obvious a lie as I ever heard. "I'll fry taters for you."

I went over to the two shaking men. They weren't fighters, you could see that.

"You better hide yourselves," I said. "It's getting awful rough."

Neither of them moved. I think they feared I was going to make a sport of them and their attempts to hide.

"As you will," I said, when they failed to move. "See what you get."

I sat on a stick chair. There were six of us in there plus the three of them. I asked my comrades who they were and the

answer was a variety. Two were Clay Countians who followed Quantrill, two were with Thrailkill, and the other,
the gray-haired reb, was with Dave Poole out of the river
district. His name was Rufus Stone.

"I weren't in it for this," he said. He seemed to have no
fear of uttering criticisms. "I have been tusslin' with these
infernal Kansans since eighteen and fifty-six. It has been a
long war for me. But I ain't in it for this."

Out of the window it all went on. Houses were plundered,
then put to the torch, and Kansas men of all descriptions shot
down.

The woman fried potatoes as we waited. The two resident
males still cowered in the corner, on the floor.

"I thought this was going to be a fight," I said.

No one replied.

Before we could eat, Pitt Mackeson and an impromptu
gang of liquored avengers rode up to the house. They wanted
to know why the place wasn't in flames.

"We're waiting on breakfast," I said. I didn't really know
these men. They were ugly drunk and had hell in their guts.
Pitt came in and saw the cowering citizens. His unlevel eyes
got big.

"Bring those men into the yard," he commanded. "I want
to show them something."

Me and Rufus Stone looked glum at each other. After a
coughing second or two he stood and said, "I think not.
We'll see to them once we've had our vittles."

"No, no you won't! I want them in the yard now, damn it!"

This springy thing happened to my legs and I found
myself standing next to Stone.

"How's it feel to want?" I asked.

Pitt Mackeson seemed rattled by my cheek. A squinty gaze was on him.

"Why, you little Dutch son of a bitch," he said. "You do what I tell you." His comrades had come up behind him and were glowering at Stone and me. "Or I'll kill you."

I put my pistol in his face as a response.

"When you figure to do this mean thing to me, Mackeson?" He backed up a step, and it was the first time I'd felt like a fighter all day. "Is this very moment convenient for you? It is for me."

Someone behind Mackeson said to just shove in there and take the men out.

"No, that won't work," Rufus Stone said. Two of the other men in the house stood to back him on that. "They're stayin' in here."

Some angry expressions got tried out on opposite audiences. I still held a tight bead on Mackeson.

"Aw, the hell with it," he said. "There's plenty other houses to burn." He turned and took a step, then whirled around on me, his long arm and a big finger aiming at my face. "I'll see you back in Missouri, you tiny sack of shit, you."

"You know where I can be found," I said.

After an unnecessary extra added look of evil, Mackeson and his crew moved on to dose out some flame.

I sat back on the stick chair and did a great, jaw-stretching false yawn.

"That man is an oaf," I said.

"That's Pitt Mackeson, ain't it?" Stone asked. "I hear he'd as soon kill a man as mash a tick."

"My, what a scary fellow he is," I said.

"Haw haw! I like you," Stone said. He clapped my shoulder. "But that bastard will have your scalp if you ain't careful, son."

"So be it," I said.

The older citizen we protected, a long-nosed skinny creature, said, "Mister, mister, there ain't enough thanks in the world."

"Aw, you go to hell!" I shouted. "Just keep your damned stinking mouth closed—you hear me?"

Well, by noon Lawrence was a charred tombstone of a place, and the scouts could see a cloud of cavalry dust buzzing toward us from the north. This made it time to go, so we did. Behind us we left a ruined settlement and a hundred fifty corpses.

Almost everybody was drunk on whiskey and bloody elation. A merchant trait had come out in the boys. There were trunks lashed ambitiously to horses, and dresses, coats, hams, rifles, whiskey, chairs, rugs and extra saddles drug along, too. We made quite a business spectacle, lugging so many oddities of supposed worth.

Not long after the sun went straight in the sky, more signs of cavalry appeared in the east. We were awful tired. The horses were jaded and the heat had risen. Now that it seemed a fight was coming our way fast, all talk of fighting was over. Flight was now the thing.

I had to always watch out for Pitt Mackeson, and I reckon I worried him some in the same regard.

The cavalry behind us gained ground. I could see them. They must've come thundering down from Leavenworth. There was enough of them, too.

The leaders said we must pick up the pace, so many of the brand-new rich had to agonize over which riches to dump when lightening their load. Greed prompts comical expressions, I noted.

Close to the Missouri border the Federals drew so near us that we halted and formed a battle line. The bluebellies did the same, and both parties just stood there staring across the field like bashful twits at a barn dance.

I think they had caught up to us only to realize that maybe that wasn't their truest desire. Both sides hooted and bleated rough appraisals of the other.

Nothing happened.

It was right after we gave up on insults and got moving again that Black John Ambrose rode alongside of me. Cave Wyatt had said that Black John killed eighteen men in Lawrence, and he looked it to me. My leader was berserk. This was troubling knowledge.

"Roedel," he said, hoarsely. "I hear disappointing words on you."

"Is that so?"

"Some of the boys tell me you spared two men you could've killed back there. Is it so?"

"Yes."

"Are you a traitor, Roedel?"

"You know I ain't."

"Well, you spared, boy. I told you not to."

I looked right at him. He might have killed me and I wanted to watch him do it.

"I know that," I said. "But I did."

He bored into me with those bottomless insane eyes. I was made nervous by his intensity, but then he said, "Don't ever disobey me again, boy. I command and you obey. That's the path to victory."

Victory, I thought. What world did he inhabit anyhow?

"I understand you," I said.

17

WITH BUSTHEAD, POPSKULL and rotgut as our scouts, we straggled home. A handful of slowpokes were caught by Federals, but for the rest of us it had been a painless foray. Not the suicide we had anticipated at all. Once we got into Cass County we dissolved into small bands. It was understood that all the armies would be after us, and we needed to hide.

I went with George Clyde, Holt, Turner Rawls, the Hudspeths, Cave Wyatt and Howard Sayles. Clyde slowly swung us to the center of the state, then up to the Big Muddy. There were still citizens there who would take us in and feed us corn cakes and rumors.

Over near Boonville we slept in a barn owned by a family named Roberts. Since the massacre an air of gloom and doom had settled over me. A number of the other boys were the same.

Howard Sayles said to me, "You did right in Lawrence, Dutchy. Me and Cave did the same, it's just no one knows it on us."

"I think I lost some comrades," I said.

It was just the three of us in the barn, and the day was sunny, the shafts of light spearing down through cracks and illuminating all the grainy debris in the air.

"Naw," said Sayles, "they lost themselves. Some of those boys are animals now."

"I'm nervous of them, too," Cave said. "This thing is only murder now. Why, Johnson Teague shot Big Bob in a argument over a bolt of cloth. They both thought *they* had stolen it." He shook his big hairy head. "It has come down to simple murder, murder on whoever is closest."

"The Jayhawkers murder, too," I said.

"That's right," Howard snapped. "But I ain't in this war to see how much like a Jayhawker I can become. I ain't fighting just to be the same as them. Now, let me tell you, Dutchy. Lots of the boys are sick about this Lawrence trip, and they're slipping down to Arkansas to join up with the regulars. What me and Cave want to know is, do you want to come?"

"When are you going?"

"Well," said Sayles, "that's not set. We might not do it. But if we do?"

"Oh, I don't know," I said. "They make you bow and scrape to officers, I hear. If I wanted to do that sort of thing, I'd just surrender."

"You know we can't surrender and live," Cave said.

"Yes, I do know that."

Sayles and Cave shook their heads at me. Cave, who I'd known long and well and joked with many a time, actually seemed sad about me. He said, "Pitt Mackeson and some of his crowd are going to kill you, Dutchy. Ain't you got no damned sense at all? You put a pistol on him and didn't use it. They're going to kill you for that."

"I been planning on trouble," I said. "But could be it'll come out different."

My comrades just stared, and by their expressions I knew that their thoughts on me all had the word *fool* in them.

Clyde kept us lollygagging around the river for a few weeks. When the big paddle boats tried to pass, we potshotted them so fiercely that they turned around. We stopped the river traffic. I always had liked these boats, and now it seemed strange that I was running them off. But war is for hurting, I guess.

Counting Holt I had two shadows. He was around me even more than he was around George Clyde. I could tell he had been changed some. The Lawrence raid made him queasy. There are lines you can't go over and come back the same.

In early October Black John called us all together. We rallied at Dover, near the river. The first thing I noticed was Pitt Mackeson watching me with a vulture visage. I gave it back to him as best I could, but he was the better at it. Cave Wyatt, Howard Sayles and Holt stayed near me, as Pitt had several constant companions of his own.

Holt, who had lethal aspects, sidled up to me.

"Jake, I could have a pistol mishap and top the man's head. You say the word and I have a streak of the terrible clumsies."

"They'd kill you on the spot, Holt. And me, too."

"Oh, yes," he said, and he grinned grimly. "But that threat is getting to be a old one."

Black John led us on a few outings into the countryside. North of the river we burned some wagons and busted up a Dutch settlement. A couple of niggers got in the way, too. All the hearts weren't in this sort of thing anymore. It was always the same men who did the murders while the rest of us went mute, but we went along.

All the gore and glory of the conflict seemed pointless. The Lawrence massacre had only prompted Order Number Eleven from the Federals. This order emptied four counties of every citizen. They just emptied those counties entirely. The newspapers carried accounts of all the rebel whippings in the east, and we could see the damage to our own state. It was only a question of how long we would go on losing before admitting we had lost. In many cases that would be forever, no matter the cost.

The boys were split now. Some comrades didn't care for others. Many were merely robbers with the bulk of numbers to back them up. To see this collapse of purpose was worse than being whipped.

George Clyde had developed into a fair-to-middling thief himself, but I knew the man well, don't you see? So I was loyal to him still. In the cold weather he took a few of us on a foray to scout places to lay up when the weather really went cold. The ground was hard and I was tired of the whole thing.

On the edge of Fire Prairie we stopped at an old gray house. We had stopped there before, and Clyde rode right up to the door in his carefree way. I was behind him with Holt and Cave. We had Yankee jackets on, and the sky was all clouds.

"Halloo in there," Clyde called out. "Mr. Mills, you in there?"

He was still smiling when the shot came. He'd been waiting for this moment, I think, and didn't even seem that surprised when it tore into his throat. He fell off his horse, gagging, and bounced on the ground.

Me and Holt jumped down to drag George back. More shots came from the house and tufted the ground around us. The other boys shot back, and me and Holt dragged our friend on out of the yard and into the trees.

One look and I knew Clyde's wound was mortal. It was the ticket to Heaven. His eyes whirled and his throat was a hole. He died quick, moist growls his last sounds.

"Oh, I can't believe this," Holt said. I don't want to tell all the emotions he showed. "I always knew him, Jake."

"It's a shame," I said. What else is there?

The boys fell back from the house. Cave Wyatt was all red in the face and puffing.

"Is George dead?" he asked.

I nodded.

"Oh, hell!" Cave exclaimed. Then he looked back to the house. "Babe is wounded. There's too many in there."

"We'll go back to Black John," I said. "All this gunfire might bring more of them around here. We ain't set up to fight them."

I strapped George across his saddle and we carried him away from that place. When we reached the main camp, a lot of the boys were saddened by the news and the proof. Clyde had been about as good and loved a fighter as there ever was.

"Where shall we bury him?" I asked Holt. No one was closer to Clyde than he was.

"We won't," he said. His expression was leveled. "I will."

With all the white fighters looking on and offering no objections, Holt mounted up and took the reins of George's horse. He loped off into the timber, no doubt searching for some flower-fat meadow or some hilltop with a precious view.

For two days Holt did not return, and when he did he failed to say a single word about where he'd been.

Two weeks later it was too cold. Groups of men split away for the winter. Several of us talked of going to Texas 'til spring. Pitt Mackeson and his crowd hooted and said they'd stick it out where the fighting was.

"That's where the plunder is, too, ain't it?" I said to Pitt.

God, he was an ugly creation.

"What of it?" he said. "You got something to make of it, Dutchy?"

I was so weary of this and him and all of it. Arch Clay was at Mackeson's side and two border buggers by the names of Dinny Riordan and Jasper Moody stood behind him.

"No," I said. "Not anymore."

Mackeson did a coyote sort of laugh and his bugger ilk joined in with him. Arch Clay stood silent as he and I were not enemies, though we had never quite been friends.

I slunk off and sat with Holt and Cave and Sayles. They were embarrassed for me.

"Tomorrow," I said. "Let's head south tomorrow."

The boys didn't respond directly, and I looked up to see Black John coming my way. As always with him, his countenance mirrored his stiff insanity. He leaned over me and said, "You have got problems in this camp, Roedel."

"So I gather."

"Well, George is dead and black in the ground by now, Roedel. He shielded you and that mute nigger, but he ain't here no more. You had best leave. Some of the boys are turned on you."

I felt myself getting weepy, though I would not weep. It had come down to this: I was being run out of a bushwhacker camp for being unsuitable.

"I'll be leaving in the morning," I said.

"Why, that'll do fine," Black John said. "Tomorrow is always a finer day, excepting in the case of my sisters. No, their tomorrow is the same as their yesterday, playing harps at the feet of Our Lord, pegging Him with peeled grapes. Yes, the sky is red tonight, Roedel, a good sign for you to go." He stood erect and clasped his hands behind his back in a schoolmarm way. "Dutchy, I don't crave seeing you dead at all. I just don't want to see you no more. I just don't want to. And when you go, you take Clyde's infernal nigger with you. I'm tired of seeing his woolly head, too."

He walked away, not expecting any retort.

Holt stared up at the sky, then lay back flat so as to view it better.

"Well, that tears that," I said sadly. I *was* a little sad. "Me and Holt'll be gone at dawn."

After a long, lonely silence, Cave said, "I'm going with you."

"I might as well come, too," Sayles said.

"Good," I told them. I looked around the camp and there were plenty of boys who didn't act like they recognized me anymore. Some of them gave me rough glances. Even the Hudspeth brothers ignored me. Turner Rawls sat with them, and when he saw me staring he got up and came over. He squatted next to me.

"I go wid oo," he mumbled. He clasped a hand on the nape of my neck and squeezed. "Yake, oo mah fwen."

"I appreciate it, Turner," I said. This man was mangle-mouthed and vicious, but he didn't forget the shared trials of past enterprises.

There was damned few that didn't.

When dawn came we were readying to go. The Mackeson crowd stood aloof from us and laughed at whispered jokes they told.

"Are you ready?" Holt asked. "I want to go."

"Well, go on," I said. "I'll only be a minute behind."

I walked into the timber and tied Old Fog to a branch. I had to get shed of yesterday's beans. It was a formidable need at the moment. I picked out a maple sapling and hunkered up against it with my britches around my ankles.

I saw Holt and the boys start off down the trail. I about strained a gut trying to be quick, but even the body some-times rebels. The job was just a slow one.

In a minute I heard boots and figured someone else shared my bean problem. Then I saw a limb shake and steel glint. As I reached into the tangle of my britches to pull loose a pistol, I got shot. It hit me in the left calf, flung my legs out from under me, and I landed squish where I didn't want to.

It hurt right away. They say it don't, but it does. It hurt. Right. Away.

"Who is it?" I screamed.

Another shot flecked bark just above me. I twisted around the tree trunk, but my leg stuck out. Someone shot at the lame thing again but missed by inches. There were more enemies than one out there.

My teeth gnashed, and I hung my pistol hand around the tree and blasted away blindly.

"Jake!" came a shout, and there was old Holt barreling over shrubs, coming in to get me. He made a pretty target while attempting such a brave move, and he paid for it. I heard that unforgettable thump and saw him slump over.

All the spirit I had sank. I pulled another pistol and emptied it without aiming, then I just lay there, loitering in my own blood and muck, awaiting the finale.

Well, old mangle-mouthed Rawls and Cave and Sayles rode up, showing more calm sense than Holt had. They winged a couple of shots at shaking shrubs and whoever had bushwhacked me took off. I wasn't too confused about who it was.

Cave looked down at me, all weepy and disgusted.

"God damn!" he said. "God damn them to hell!"

All my thoughts were simple and focused on pain. This thing, pain, is a commanding sensation.

A rag was bound about the wound and I was hoisted to my horse. I didn't want to see my leg. If it resembled Jack Bull's elbow in any particulars, I preferred not to know it.

Turner got Holt over to us. He was in the saddle but gasping. The breath had been blown out of him. There was blood seeping out low in his ribs.

"Are you bad?" Sayles asked him.

"It rattled the ribs, but they are stout," Holt said tightly. "The ball didn't go in. It's only the skin is torn."

Cave was still having a hissy fit and pointed toward the camp.

"I'd go after them, Jake," he said. "I truly would, but I'm afraid that might just be exactly what they want."

"Oh, no, to hell with that," Sayles said. "There'll be time for that another day. Right now we got to get Dutchy and Holt to my father-in-law's place. Dutchy's fiancée is there and she'll tend to them."

"His fiancée," Cave said. "What fiancée?"

"That Sue Lee Shelley girl. She is Dutchy's fiancée."

"Oh. Oh, her."

And we set off.

18

THREE DAYS LATER, or so I suppose, we were there. The house was a sturdy wood one far in the hills. My mind had been on a float as we traveled. Some things I had understood. I suspect I yowled too much.

When we arrived it was late in the day. The boys helped me hop into the house. There was an old man, built thinly and bald, inside. This was Orton Brown, Howard Sayles's father-in-law. His wife was a feminine replica of him except in regards to hair. Her name was Wilma.

"Who is this?" Orton asked Sayles.

"This is Dutchy Roedel. He's been tweaked in the leg."

"Oh, so that's Dutchy Roedel. Well, lay him down."

Holt flopped down next to me. He was somewhat grayed by his wound but not in danger of dying. Exhaustion played a big part in how he looked.

The hole in my calf itched and ached, but the bone was not shattered. That gave me confidence that my future might be a walking one. Cave Wyatt had shown off his nursing qualities and kept the thing clean and bandaged. Holt could reach his own wound and tend it, as it was mainly a bruise and a rip, so he did.

"I appreciate this of you," I said to Orton.

"Well, I have heard of you and I am proud to help a southern man no matter how funny his name."

"Oh, he ain't just a southern man, Ort," Sayles said. "This boy here is the Shelley girl's fiancé."

Orton raised his brows at this news.

"Good, good. I am glad to hear she has a fiancé, 'cause she is in need of one."

"Hey, now," I said. "I never told you I was her fiancé."

That got me a cruel expression from Sayles.

"Aw, goin' back to your old tricks, eh, Dutchy?" he said, then gave a soft kick at my calf. "She's with child and you want to quibble."

"She ain't with child," Orton said.

"That is for certain," said Wilma in a stern Baptist tone. "That girl has *got* child now. A brown-eyed butterball of a girl child."

When I heard that, I wanted to see that baby. I had a real need to study the face of Jack Bull's child and dote on any resemblance.

"Where is she?" I asked. "Where is Sue Lee and the baby?"

"I'm not for sure," Wilma said. "I believe she carried the little girl out for air. They'll be back any time, now. They won't stay out in the dark."

From the house I had a view of a steep hillside, thick with oak and hickory, and a deep, clean streamed valley. It was a soothing landscape and one that made me feel safe. For the first time in a long while, I could relax and leave it to nature to concoct my cure.

Orton and Wilma and the boys jawed around as the sun went behind the hill. Howard Sayles's wife was in Hillsboro, Texas, with his father and mother and two children. The Browns had news from there, so they shared it.

Me and Holt were off to one side of the conversation. This conflict had forced us to rely on each other, and we had learned to do it. I felt obliged toward this particular nigger. He had demonstrated backbone and superb nerve. I hoped I had done the same.

"After we get healed back healthy, what shall we do, Holt?"

"More, I reckon," he answered. He did not face me when he said it, and it may not have been true.

"Uh-huh," I said, harnessing my own thoughts. "More is right, but could be it'll be more of something else. I ain't riding with boys that'll shoot me no more. Them days is gone."

He nodded briskly several times.

"You got yourself a new family now," he said. "I understand it that you don't want to bushwhack no more."

I'll tell you, odd events at which I had been a mere witness were now conspiring to manage my fate, and I wasn't used to having so little say.

"Now, Holt, that ain't my kid and you know it."

"It ain't that simple," he said, all puffed up with mysterious logic. "What you say is the truth, far as that goes, but it is too simple. And this ain't that simple."

I guess I have myself to blame. I listened to him. Then I sat there, throbbing at my wounded calf, somewhat absent of insight, and pondered his riddle.

★   ★   ★

When she come in, she reacted like she had seen me at the waterhole yesterday. Zero fluster came over her face. She was calm and beautiful in her scar-faced way, serene with motherhood, I supposed.

"Are you hurt *again?*" she asked me.

Those were her first words to me. They did not flatter me with a gush of feminine concern.

"Well, yes," I said, "but I didn't do it to myself, you know." I conjured up a forlorn look. "I been shot."

She clucked her tongue and swung the cuddly armful of babe that she carted.

"Bushwhackers have to expect that," she said. She then smiled a wide one and sat next to me. The baby murmured and Sue Lee actually leaned over and kissed my forehead like she had the right. "It is good to see you, Jake. And you, too, Holt."

"I hear you saying it," I whimpered. My expectations had not been specific, but warmth and concern had been in them all. "Let me see that baby."

"Proud to," she said, and you could tell by her rosy visage that it was true. Man, nature has some changes in store for us all, and it had worked a good one on her. "Her name is Grace Shelley Chiles as far as I'm concerned."

Babes don't know anything but nipples and lullabies. They splash out looks of wonder on anybody whether they merit it or not. This one was the same, and when Sue Lee handed the seedling creature to me it did a tiny paw grab at my lips, gurgling like it knew me. Grace had eyes that leaned toward brown, and several soft wattles on her face that would harden into features.

"She is wonderful," I said.

"She real pink," Holt said. He then touched her quickly, and when nothing wrong came of that gesture he did it again, only this time his touch lingered. A big smile was on his face. "Babies is something I never can believe."

"What do you mean?" I asked.

"Well, *look* at it," he said. "Do you believe that thing will shout and holler and haul water someday?"

To realize that this little handful was actually a person is to have faith in a miracle of dimensions. I admit that.

"I know what you mean," I said. I placed Grace on the floor beside me and grinned at Momma. "She is sweet."

"I know it," she said. She then began to poke at my wound, her brow all scrunched up. "Let me see your bad spot, Jake. I want to make sure it's clean."

"It's clean enough," I said.

She shook her head and said, "No, Jake. Clean enough ain't good enough. You should have learned that."

I was real stoked up with feelings. I guess I wanted to be cared for. Anyway, I settled back and let her do it.

Turner, Cave and Sayles rested themselves for a few days. Sayles wanted to go join his wife and children in Texas before heavy winter was full upon us.

"You can stay here with Ort as long as you like," Sayles said to me. "Him and Wilma have taken a shine to Sue Lee and the tiny critter."

"My leg is fairly useless for now," I said. "I don't know what to do."

"Aw," Cave said, "get yourself well, then join us in Texas. There'll be interesting things to do in Texas."

"Lahk wha?" Turner asked. It was one of his rare comments. He seemed to hate speaking in his blubbery manner around women.

"Well, now," Cave said. "There is Mexico nearby Texas. Lots of land down there and no one to claim it."

"There's Mexicans down there," I said. "Quite a few of them, too, from what I hear."

"Oh, all right. Certainly there are Mexicans down there, Dutchy. But damned few white men."

"That sound like another fight," Holt said.

"Probably," Cave responded. "Probably there would be a fight. But it'd be a fight for a new start. That's a different thing."

"Will you go to Mex?" I asked Sayles.

"I don't plan on it," he said. "I only want to see my wife and kids in Texas."

Turner Rawls cackled and snorted rudely.

"Oh, hell wid dis. Ah jine Bock Yawn." He stared at me, the rude look still on his face. "Oo mah fwen, Yake. Ah hep oo bud now Ah jine Bock Yawn."

I looked at his badly angled jaw, and pondered his haphazard speech. We had been together in several hot spots, but the string was played out.

"Are you sure you want to do that?" I asked.

He nodded.

"Dis mah war heah."

I think his comment soured Cave and Sayles. I reckon it made us all feel a bit like skulkers. I know this: the conversation dwindled and we all leaned back in the shadows of the room, lost in individual thoughts of the future, and I don't guess the whole gang of us showed up in any of them.

On the morning after, the boys took off by different routes, Cave and Sayles heading south to new things and Turner trotting north for more of the old.

It made me and Holt sad, but Sue Lee and Grace settled next to us, and their mere presence lifted the gloom.

"I have a thing or two to say to you, Jake," Sue Lee said.

There was a cock crowing nearby, and a bright day of light was coming around. Wilma was rustling up some oatmeal and Orton was out tending the horses. I had a very contented feeling everywhere but in my calf.

"Well, speak up," I said.

"I think I want a walk," Holt said. He raised himself and walked weakly to the door. Banged-up ribs are slow to mend. "This ain't my business."

"Jake," Sue Lee said when we were alone. "What's this trash I hear about you being my fiancé?"

She had that mess of hair of hers hanging wild over her face, but it had a rough charm to it. Her skin was clear and pink and healthy. I guess I did like her pretty well despite some things.

"Oh. So you have heard that. Well, it was sprung on me by Sayles." I tried a bashful smile on her. "See, they all thought you was carrying my kid 'cause I brung you into camp after, you know, Jack Bull."

"Ah," she said, and reared her head way back so she could study me and her nose in one glance. "Do you figure I ought to be married?"

"Yes, if you want to keep fingers from wagging in your face."

"Oh, that doesn't bother me."

"Well, it's also another thing, Sue Lee. They got a name for kids without daddies, you know. It's not a good one."

"I know that. So, do *you* want to marry me, Jake?"

"Naw. Not too bad."

"Good. That's good news. I wouldn't marry you for a wagonload of gold."

"I'll bet you wouldn't."

"I wouldn't."

"I'll just bet you wouldn't."

Grace was on the floor between us, flinging her hands and feet around like a back-rolled turtle.

"I wouldn't marry you even if you weren't a runty Dutchman with a nubbin for a finger."

"Fine," I said hotly. "That's damned fine. I wouldn't want a wife who didn't have whole teeth. Anyhow, being your man is bad luck. I don't need to marry any of that."

That comment wobbled her fine face. Her hands went clawing through her hair.

"Well, it's true," she said. "I guess it's true. That's why I won't hook up with any more fighters. I just won't do it."

I knew I was somewhat mean as well as a liar. That is the way of the cautious heart.

"You're not bad luck," I said. "You have had bad luck, that's all."

When I speak nice I suppose it don't sound quite authentic. She faced down, her eyes on the flopping baby, and shook her head.

"I'd need convincing that you mean that," she said. "Then I'd need convincing that you were right."

I went on the mend in the following weeks. The wound no longer hurt too much, but the leg wobbled when I put weight on it.

The days at Orton Brown's had a routine to them. Orton, who I had grown fond of, rose each morning in time to mock the cockcrow. He slopped his hogs and tended the horses, and by the time that was done Wilma had a breakfast ready.

After eating, I would languish at the sunniest window and Holt would go for a long walk, no matter the weather. Generally I would be stuck with Grace while Sue Lee pitched in with Wilma at whatever chores the day required. I tried corraling the babe on my sunny bit of floor, but she did baby things. The floor was dirty and splintery and new to her, so she licked at it. She tried crawling away at my every unaware moment and drove me cranky and practical right quick. I took a lash of rope and tied one end to my ankle and noosed the other on her leg and gained a moment of peace for myself. The kid, anchored or no, pitched out bawling sounds worse than a gut-shot Yank on a real hot day. I never did anything to provoke these bellows, but once Sue Lee walked by in the midst of one and said, "Sweet thing wants some suck, but Momma is busy."

I understand what that meant well enough, but I knew that I could not duplicate the feat. A man just ain't a mother and that's all there is to it. But the next time she went into an infant rant, I had that in mind. I tried manly angles of diversion on the child. I crooned raspy lullabies and made carnival faces and attempted various unlearned tricks. None of it worked. The tiny face stayed soured up and the bawling became desperate.

I picked Grace up after all her squally prompting. To caress or strangle her was the question in my mind. I swung her about, swaying on my gimpy leg, hoping movement and embrace might calm her. It didn't, so I ran my free hand over her cheeks to pinch them and my nubbin passed those infant lips and she clamped right onto it. She went silent on the instant and gummed away at that nubbin. My stump was exactly acceptable to a cantankerous babe after suck.

I staggered on one wound and soothed with another.

It was the sudden silence I reckon that brung Sue Lee into the room, her eyes all suspicious. She watched my soothing exercise for a moment, not too thrilled with it, and said, "I suppose I'll feed her."

"Hell, no, you won't," I said. "I've just now got this thing under control."

"She needs to be suckled, Jake."

I gimped back toward the front room with old spoilsport giving chase. I turned away from her, and as she turned after me my leg gave out and I about fell. I wouldn't want to hurt the babe for anything, so I had to give her up to Momma.

"Here now," Sue Lee said. She sat in a chair by the window and cradled Grace to her chest. I was standing right there, but she unbuttoned her blouse and let a big pink-nippled breast flop out. Seeing one gave me a good notion of how the pair would look. She just stared right at me, a saucy, sassy gleam to her eyes, as Grace slurped after suck.

I collapsed to the floor. This business had always been kept private before. The scene this process made sort of jolted me. I had to watch it. That woman had a holy expression on her face that most any god would covet.

I slid across the floor to get closer. I sat at her feet and intently studied the effect of a nipple on a suckling child. Sue Lee studied me about as intently, but she didn't turn away and she didn't say scat.

My nature really rose seeing her that way. Probably it shouldn't have, but, mister, it did.

At night Holt and me stretched out on the floor. I could tell by the way he breathed that he was awake. It had gotten to where sleep didn't lead to rest. I suppose that after some weeks of safety, grief and shudders had caught up to us.

When I reckoned myself to be in slumber, a number of rude deeds were embellished in dreams. I had a glimpse of the black tongues on the hanged. Whole sequences of pistols and bloodied heads played out. Jack Bull Chiles tried to peel an apple with only one arm and a dripping stump. This one thing hit me over and over: a smart sprout of a Dutch boy being back-shot. And on one night of fevered fictions, Pitt Mackeson slinked up to finish the job on me.

This startled me awake. I sat up.

"Can't sleep?" Holt asked.

"Naw. These quilts are too heavy. They make me sweat."

"Mine, too."

There were also the live nightmares to occupy my thoughts. Orton had gotten in the habit of relaying rumors about the boys and Black John. He said they were being hurt by the Federals but still did some fighting, a lot of robbing and too much scalping. He had claimed that Black John was dead, but I didn't think it was so. I could well believe that the Cause had been set loose in the lust for loot. Anyone could have seen it coming.

I wondered if all the war I had slopped through had gone for naught, so I said to Holt, "Holt, was all that fighting for naught?"

I lit a candle while I waited on his answer.

"How would I know?" he said. The little flame flickered and did shadowy things on our faces. "What it is I do know is all them dead niggers in Lawrence. I can't toss them dead niggers out of my mind."

"It was a lot of dead types in Lawrence," I said.

"They didn't spare a single nigger."

"They didn't *want* to spare anybody, Holt."

"Jake, what I think of the boys is this: niggers and Dutchies is their special targets. Why was we with them?"

"Why, to stop the Yankee aggressors."

"But we didn't stop them."

"No."

"And the boys shot you and the boys shot me."

"That was personal," I said. "Personal ain't war."

Holt chewed on that for a moment. He had a proud look on his face, and I knew he was lost for what to do next.

"George is dead, Jack Bull is dead, Riley is dead and Pitt Mackeson is alive. Now, where does that leave you and me, Jake? Where does that leave me?"

This was one of those times I was supposed to have an answer. But there was no revelations on my side of the candle neither, so I said, "Right here, Holt."

He did a stretched-lip look of disgust. I guess I was a disappointment.

"I knew we were here," he said. "And this ain't nowhere for me."

Later on Holt snored and I didn't. I took a candle and slid over the floor to my satchel. I had an errand to do and I needed my writing implements to bring it off.

For an address I put down "The Bull Family of Frankfort, Kentucky."

Dear Mother and Missus Chiles, I wrote. I hope this letter finds you. I am only guessing as to where you are. Missus Chiles, will you please read this to Mother?

There is sad news. Jack Bull is dead, slain by the invaders, as was his father before him. The thing to say is he died for his nation I guess. Actually a doctor might have staved off infection, but there was none and this laid him low. He made as dignified a passing as was possible and there is no reason to be anything but proud of him. I loved him as a brother and you know it.

Mother, Father's death torments me so. I know I gave him

little but argument. His fascination with General Sigel and all things Federal never took hold in me. I gave him grief for that. I still believe he is wrong; we don't have to tolerate invaders just because they have uniforms and high-sounding titles. That is an Old World trait and I won't have it. But I never wanted Father hurt over me. We all walked in the dark. I feel I killed him in too many ways. I won't babble off the whole long list of my regrets.

I hope to someday see you both again. It would be best in a peaceful spot, but it would be good anywhere. I don't think it will happen soon.

There is one more thing, and I say it only in confidence, and solely to give hope. Jack Bull fathered a girl child last winter and she is a close image of him. I will try to care for the babe as much as fortune allows, for Jack Bull would wish it of me.

I have too much more to say to say anything.

I am wounded somewhat and where I am headed is unknown. It probably won't be where you are. With all my regards, Jacob.

19

WHEN THE SUN slipped up I was waiting on it. Orton came from his bedroom, rubbing the yellow crud from the corners of his eyes. He carried his boots and sat next to me to put them on.

"How you feeling, Dutchy?"

"Not so bad."

"You look like you feel good. Do you feel good?"

"I don't feel too bad."

"Ah," he went, then pulled on his boots. "You seem about healed up to me."

"It still hurts some, my leg does."

"But it's about healed, ain't it?"

"I suppose so," I said. "Why are you so curious, Ort?"

He cocked his head and shrugged.

"Just enjoy it to see a man get well, Dutchy. That's all."

I watched him go to the kitchen, and he came back quick, gnawing on a piece of corn bread.

"I got to go to Hartwell today," he said. "I should be back by night."

"You want me to come along?" I asked.

"Naw. You go on and finish healing. I'll take the nigger with me, though. He's a handy gunman, I hear tell."

"That's true," I said. "Post this letter for me, would you?"

He nodded and took the note when I handed it to him. He put it inside his shirt.

I shoved Holt awake. His eyes were all bloody and he didn't seem too well rested.

"Mr. Brown wants you to ride with him to Hartwell, Holt."

"What? All right," he said. In about a minute he was ready to go.

Orton grabbed his shotgun and he and Holt went to saddle up. I wobbled out to watch them leave. It was a cold morning, and there had been a smearing of snow in the night. My lungs welcomed the clean, chilled air.

The men rode from the barn past the porch where I stood. "You get on in and rest, now," Orton said. "I want you rested, Dutchy."

"I guess I'll do that," I said, but I stayed right there and watched them amble off over the thin snow and hard earth, out of sight.

During the day I did my normal thing. That is, I cornered gurgly Grace on a blanket on the floor and just reveled in that child. My confusion amongst babes had lessened tremendously when I'd learned that my nubbin could calm them at their stormiest.

Sue Lee seemed worried I might spoil Grace. She was always saying, "It is time for her nap" or "Don't fling her in the air thataway, Jake!" Mothers are endless with those comments.

After the noon meal Sue Lee suckled Grace. This was my favorite part of the day. I watched, and it could be I *over*-watched, for Mommy's cheeks reddened.

"Are you always going to stare like that?" she asked me.

"Long as I can."

"Well, you're pretty near well, so it won't be much longer." She turned away from me slightly. "I reckon you and Holt'll be off to get shot by some *different* fellows here pretty soon."

That was a prediction that could come true. Bodily calamities just seemed to be in the cards. But I thought I was about done with bushwhacking gangs, and the regular Confederates had too many rules. None of that interested me. I was still loyal to the Cause but leery of the people.

"Maybe I won't," I said.

"What will you do, then?"

"Oh, now maybe I'll trek on over to California and catch me a sailboat to somewhere sunny and full of lambs."

"Is that right," she said and laughed. "What grand spot have you got in mind, Jake?"

The baby gummed away at the nourishing breast, and I stretched my legs out straight and leaned back on my hands.

"In Sparta they have olives," I said. "I got that out of a book. I could eat me some olives, I think."

"Olives? What are olives like?"

"Well, I don't know firsthand. I never had one yet. But I've eat a bushel of walnuts, and nothing can be more trouble to eat than them."

A look of deep thought came over Sue Lee's face. She switched Grace to the spare nipple, her fingers moving fast, then sighed as the babe went to work.

"I wonder about me," she said. "I ain't going sailing nowhere and I know it. I wonder about me and Grace."

"Oh, you'll get by," I said. That was all the honesty I could summon. I hate it when they put you on the spot. I don't like lying, but I hate it worse when I don't tell the truth. "You know, that girl needs her a daddy."

"She had a daddy, Jake, and you ain't it."

That comment was uncalled for. I pushed myself to my feet and pointed a finger in her face.

"You know, girl," I said all hot and breathy. "You're going to have to get your water from the nearest well, or else learn to love lugging that *heavy bucket* of yours."

And with that I went outside and stood beneath a sky of gray, trembling in my effort to rein myself in from becoming a mushmouth.

That girl was starting to bring it out in me.

Late in the afternoon I noted two things: Wilma dusted off the family Bible and put it on the table; then she baked bread and tommyhawked a chicken though it wasn't Sunday.

"What's with the special favors, Wilma?" I asked.

Now, this was an older lady and she gave me an older-lady look of shrewdness.

"Why, nothing," she said. "Orton will be mighty hungry from the ride, don't you think? I intend to feed him well."

Uh-huh, I thought.

In an hour or so Orton and Holt rode up with a fat, pale, dark-dressed stranger. I watched them from the window, and when they came in the stranger looked at me and said, "Is this the man?"

"That's him," Orton said. "Dutchy Roedel."

Holt stood in the doorway, trying to choke down some sniggers.

"What is this?" I asked.

"This is Reverend Horace Wright," Orton said. He held his shotgun by the barrel with the butt on the floor. "You're getting married today, Dutchy. You're getting married or you're getting out."

"I'm what?"

"You heard me. You're all healed. I wanted to be sure you wouldn't die slow before I did this. I can't have it in my house the way it is."

Wilma bustled Sue Lee into the room. I guess she was about as rattled by this as me, but she sure didn't look it.

"Holt, saddle my horse," I said. I was all puffed with myself, like the rooster in a one-rooster county. "We're getting out of here."

"No, no," he said. He shook his head several times, and I wanted to pop him in the middle of his grin. "You should do right, Jake."

"What on earth does that mean?" I screamed.

The reverend chewed his lips and looked on me without too much pity. Orton matched him and the place went silent. Sue Lee poked me in the ribs with a finger and nodded toward the porch.

"Let's talk," she said.

"I do believe that is a roasting chicken I smell," the reverend said.

Me and the widow marched outside. I did stuttery steps and bashful coughs while this girl, who had been here before, stared at me sternly. Hell, I'd never even whispered sweet folderol to a maiden I'd liked, let alone got legally trussed up with a widow.

"Are you going to or not?" she asked. "Be forthright."

"It's being shoved down my throat," I said. "If a thing has got to be shoved, I like to do the shoving."

She smirked at me, and for an instant there I had a good idea of how she came by that busted tooth.

"Well, get on in there and shove, then, Jake."

I sat on the lip of the porch and rested my leg. It was more than chilly and the sun was sinking.

"I thought you said you wouldn't want me for a wagon-load of gold 'cause I am a nubbin-fingered runt of a Dutchman. I remember you saying that."

"Well," she said, brightly, "I guess I lied."

"Are you lying again now?"

"No. I wouldn't lie to you, Jake."

"You just told me you lied to me before."

"That's different," she said. "That was romance."

"And now is what?"

She touched my forehead and curled an arm around my neck. "Now is the truth." She then eased my face to her feeders, and twirled a finger in my hair. "This here now is the truth."

The truth made my face flush. I was glad it was hidden from her.

"Jack Bull would want that girl to have a daddy," I said. "He was like my brother. I guess I'll do it."

Reverend Wright was hungry, and from the pudgy look of him he wasn't one to put up with that. He did a lickety-split ceremony and sniffed the chicken-soaked air like some ridiculous hound.

Bachelorhood vanished in a blink, and Holt slammed my back, and Wilma beamed. There was a load of righteous happy stuff done. I stood up to it and Sue Lee stood up to it and, hell, it didn't hurt or nothing.

I thought to ask Orton what sect this reverend headed.

"Oh, he is Methodist, but he marries all breeds."

The reverend was over at the table, his haunches jiggling, ripping off chunks of bread and mashing his mouth.

"I reckon that man would marry stones to stones if there was a chicken at the end of it," I said.

"That's neither here nor somewhere else," Orton said. "He done made you legal."

Pretty soon we all sat down and tore up the bird and bread, and Orton hauled out a jug in honor of the occasion. Reverend Wright said he was opposed to drinking but for us to please go on. I guess gluttony is not so bad so long as you don't double up on your vices by washing it down with something tasty.

The rest of us mumbled a few toasts, and Sue Lee got her share. The girl liked her drink fairly well for a girl. It charged her face with rosy attitudes.

I liked that.

After all these gestures things slid back into the normal way. Orton and Wilma retired early, then Sue Lee and Grace did the same. The reverend sacked out on the floor where Holt and me had been sleeping. The man had several pistols on him, as he was aware that the Lord works in mysterious ways and some of them require the blasting of others.

"You a family man now," Holt said to me. "How do you feel?"

"I feel the same, Holt." I sat beside him on the floor, back to the wall. "Hell, it's only words."

"No. It's a oath, Jake. That's words that you got to back up."

"Oh, I know that," I said. Holt pulled his blanket over himself and started to curl up. "I reckon we'll be hauling her and the kid with us now."

"Where to?"

"I don't know. Out of here. Maybe Utah Territory."

Holt lay there watching me, a puzzled look on his face. I pulled my boots off and spread my bedroll and lay down, then Holt sat up.

"What you doing?" he asked me.

"I am going to sleep. You gone blind? I am fixing to get me some sleep."

His lower jaw dropped, and he shook his head so hard his cheeks flapped.

"Jake, do I got to tell you this?"

"Tell me what?"

"You *s'posed* sleep with the wife, Jake. For pity sake, you got to know that much. You *s'posed* to share her bed, that way some other man ever do that you shoot him, 'cause that be *your* place by *oath*."

"I know all that," I said. "You bet I know that. But hell, this ain't some regular marriage situation."

"Don't you like her?" Holt pulled the blanket up over his knees as if settling in for a long spell of chat. "You ain't gonna lie to me that you don't."

"I like her," I said, and felt dazed by the admission. "She's pretty enough and all that, but this thing marriage has swept over me so sudden."

"Well, Jake," Holt said in his somber tone, "it *is* over you. I mean, you done did the milkin', might as well lap the cream."

I gazed about the room and watched the swelling and sinking of the preacher's form as he sawed away, and moonlight leaked in the window with the hue of some weak gold. Holt was all eyes watching me and I was mostly nerves myself.

I grabbed my boots and slinked away. Sue Lee had a room off the kitchen, and I crept to the door. My heart was kicking up its heels and slamming hell out of my ribs.

I creaked the door open slow, and there she was, stretched out with her eyes closed and a candle burning nearby.

As I stepped into the room she opened her eyes and said, "Jake."

Grace was asleep in a tiny rocking contraption Orton had built. She was drawing pure, sleepy breaths.

I dropped my boots and tossed my hat on top of them. I put my pistols down.

The candle burned on a side table, and she sat up in bed, wearing some garment that left her shoulders bare. There was a vastness of skin showing.

For a second I fumbled with the button on my britches, then thought better of it and started into bed.

"Hey," she said with a long soft drawl, "take your clothes off." There was a glow to her and some smiley expectations played out on her face. "You don't come to bed in dirty duds, Jake. Now, that's a rule."

Well, I just stood there, which is one of my favorite poses, as whenever I hear the mention of a rule my first urge is to find it and give it a shake. This trait had never made my life easier, and it didn't do it now.

"Just how many rules is it you've got lined up for me, girl?"

"Oh, don't get mad." She swung out of bed and bare-footed over to me, and, damn, there wasn't a gnat's width of cotton between her and nakedness. "I'll help you." She jerked my shirt over my head, then reached to my button and undid it. My britches dropped. That left me bare-assed in front of this creature, and this was a new feature to my life. It brought some tingles with it.

"There," she said. She stood right before me, hands on her hips, mocking my Christian rearing, her lips splayed in a bold smile, then whisked that veil of cotton from her form.

"Oh!" I went.

She sat on the bed next to me and did a spitty kiss on my ear. There was a thicket of hair on her south forty, and I'll tell you I'd never plowed through any of that so I edged my hand down there and felt of it.

"Huh," she said, her breath whistling on my neck as my hands did clumsy things. "Are you virgin?"

"I've sinned plenty," I told her.

"But have you ever bedded a woman before?"

"Girl, I've killed fifteen men."

I dropped my good hand between her legs, then slithered those fingers about. She went "Mmmm," so I poked her with a finger in that place where a woman can best stand it. I kept the poke steady in there but remained seated.

"You ain't too shy, are you?" she asked me.

"I want to go about it right."

"Well, right or wrong, honey, go on and go about it."

I did not care for her tone, but my savories began to swell. I started to swirl with my finger as though it were a sapling twig in a creek eddy.

She liked this.

Things got wet, and my nature sprang straight up, and this widow, my wife, eased me onto my back and shuffled on top of me and we kissed the longest one I'd ever gone through.

And one thing led to another.

20

THE NEXT TWO weeks wisped along, with me shambling through them in a fog. Sue Lee gave me nightly lessons in gaiety. I found I took to this form of learning fairly well.

After those two weeks of rigorous instruction, I got antsy to travel. It was funny how quickly I felt healed. I was rowdy with health.

One morning I just came out with it and said, "It's time to go to Texas. The roads are clear."

"There's a lot of bad sorts between here and Texas," Orton said. "If you ain't shot *for* a thief, you'll be shot *by* a thief."

"Maybe not," Holt said somewhat ominously. I knew he was ready to go, and had been for a while.

The wife I had got me didn't say anything, but I knew it wasn't a strange notion to her. I had babbled about Texas in soft, naked moments, and said how I wanted a place for her and the girl. I made it clear that I was done with fighting, at least I was done with this fight 'til it spread to Texas.

"Tomorrow," she said. "Tomorrow would be a good day to go."

That settled it. Several things had to be done, though, and

one of them was for me to give up my rebel locks. With bushwhacker curls hanging past my shoulders, it would be hard for me to lie about some things if trouble rolled up on us. All that hair was part of a dread costume, and I had to get shorn of it.

Orton did the shearing and displayed some gusto about the enterprise. He snipped my locks so near my ears I thought he left me looking moonfaced and childlike.

"Dutchy," he said, "you look twenty-one again."

"I'm just now nineteen, Ort."

"Oh. Is that right? Well, you'll never look that young."

All around my boots there were long strands of pale hair, the ornamentation of my rebellion, and seeing them on the floor made me wistful.

"We said we'd never cut our hair 'til we were finished with the war."

"And you didn't, Dutchy. You didn't."

We passed one more night with the Browns of Henry County, Missouri. At dawn Wilma gave us a starter sack of provisions. She doted on Grace and said several times she would pray for us all. Orton shook my hand about every sixth minute and told me to be careful, like this was my first trip from home.

I did not relish the prospect of saying good-bye. The actual moment of farewell was a damp one. Wilma trickled and Sue Lee bawled. My wife had grown so close to this thinned-out old pair. The whole thing made her sad.

It couldn't be helped.

"So long," I said, and we went.

Our journey was to be a long one, and this region was writhing with robbers and rebels and scavengers and Yanks. It was hard circumstances under which to embark on a marriage. Holt and me reverted quick to our old, wary style, and Sue Lee loped along on Jack Bull's horse, Grace strapped to her back.

Knowing we were leaving Missouri and my hard-fought-for home shuddered me with emotions. Everything I had ever known had been learned here. I knew I was not a quitter, but I was quitting this place. I guess that's putting too fine a point on things. I did not like being run from my home, but now I wondered if it ever had been that. Boys do the quickest thing that comes to mind, and for me that had been to side with Jack Bull and rebellion, even against my own father and his ilk. From loyalty to a man, I would have murdered a people.

All this brought back an old taste for piety in me.

As we traveled south, we avoided everybody we could. All the elusive bushwhacker skills Holt and me knew were employed to dodge Gray patrols and Blue patrols and clumps of barefoot refugees. I had a family to convoy and they didn't need to learn how trouble feels close up and sudden.

South of El Dorado Springs Holt engaged me in talk.

"Jake, I do a lot for you, you know that?"

"You know I do. It's equal."

"Oh, don't say it, Jake. I got to say a thing." His face was composed and firm with decision. I saw him in this good posture and thought, Mister, we have done some things together, this man and me. "Jake, I'll travel with you and yours 'til we past them Pin Indians and riffraff in the Nation, then I got to go off somewhere."

"Where? Where will you go?"

"I ain't decided that to a definite aim. But I'm going."

"Why?"

Holt swiveled his stare to my wife and the child, then looked at me like I was once more a fool, and said, "Now, come on! What you mean, *why?*"

Oh, I was weary of vanishing comrades, but I understood it.

"Good luck, Holt. I wish you well and more."

"It ain't yet," he said. "I ain't leaving you 'til your little Dutch ass past them Pin Indians. I told you that, didn't I?"

Sue Lee was an uncomplaining traveler. She shouldered every hardship and asked no special favors. Near Newport we awoke at sunrise and built a fire to boil chicory. I let her take charge of the task, and before long the pot gave out a good smell.

Naturally I had heard that my old comrades were stamping through this neighborhood, but when I heard a rattle and turned to see Arch Clay pointing a pistol at me, it was still a shocking reunion.

"Why, Dutchy," he said. He holstered his pistol and stepped closer. "I didn't expect to see you no more."

Me and Holt looked tight at each other. I think it occurred to both of us that killing Arch right off might be the wisest course. But we hesitated.

"Chicory is boiling, Arch," I said. "Have some."

"I think I will," he said. He dragged his horse in and I saw evidence of new habits, for there were three scalps dangling from the bridle reins. "I think I'd like some chicory, Dutchy. How you, Holt?"

"Fairly well," Holt said.

"Are you alone, Arch?" I asked.

"Naw," he said. This man had never looked angelic, but now he appeared totally won over to the devil's side. "Two of the boys are back a ways. We been on the run sort of constant."

"How is Black John?"

Arch shrugged.

"That's a big question, Dutchy, 'cause the man is dead. Black John is dead. Who ain't? They got him at Dover and stuck his head on a pole and paraded it down the streets. They put a picture of it in their paper." He looked me in the eye. "It's been rough times for us who stuck it out."

"Aw, the war is lost," I said.

"No shit, Dutchy. Who does this gal and kid belong to?"

"That's my wife."

"Huh. If that don't beat all. *You* got a wife and I *don't*."

A thin trail of mud ran a few feet east of us. I hoped there would be no trouble, and tended to the chicory as I waited.

"Where you headed?" I asked.

"Newport."

"Hell, man, the militia is in Newport. You can't go in there."

"Wrong," Arch said. "I am goin' in there." He seemed

way gone in spirit, forlorn and fearless. "I'm for certain sure goin' in there. I want a drink. They have drinks in Newport. Whiskey. Lager. I want some of both."

"Arch, they'll kill you. There's a couple hundred of them. You need to clear out of this country."

"I don't think so, Dutchy. I don't reckon I'll clear out of where I was born. I believe I just won't do it. That there is my hometown. I was raised in there, and I reckon I'll go on in and have me a drink there, too. Maybe more than one. Maybe a thousand."

"They'll kill you sure."

"Oh, oh," he said and his lips turned up sickly. "What a horrible fate. Haw, haw, haw. Yes, a horrible fate."

His whole attitude made me nervous. Sue Lee gave me several shaky glances, and Holt looked down the trail.

"Riders," Holt said.

"That'll be the boys," Arch said. "We all three decided today was the sort of day when we just had to have a drink in Newport."

Holt and me stood, and I stepped into the timber to see which boys it was. When I saw them clear, I drew a pistol. One was good old Turner Rawls, but the other was Pitt Mackeson.

Both of their bridles flew scalps.

"It's Mackeson," I said to Holt.

Holt unlimbered his arms and Arch continued to just sit there, blowing on his chicory.

"Mackeson!" I shouted. I stepped to where he could see me, and when he did he drew.

I shot first and not well. He spurred his horse into the timber on the other side of the trail, and I snuggled behind a stout log on my side. I kept looking for Arch to come up behind me, but he never moved.

Mackeson shot into my general neighborhood and I paid him back in kind. Turner seemed to take no notice of the gunfire and rode on up to me.

"Yake," he said.

"Get out of the way, Turner." I prayed that this mangle-mouthed comrade wouldn't make me kill him. My entire life, such as it had been, narrowed down to this instant.

"Yake, he kill oo."

"Get out of the way, Turner!"

Off to the side of my vision I saw Arch stand. Holt covered him with a pistol.

"Arch, don't get in it."

Arch shook his head, all stolid and mysterious, then walked right past Holt and onto the trail. He mounted his horse.

"Come on, Rawls," he said. Then he looked to where I lurked. "Dutchy, we're goin' on to Newport. Don't be a fool and keep up at this shootin' business."

My wife had been hurled into a mood. She staggered about, with Grace in her hands, crying, and shouting a chorus of premature bereavement, "Oh, no, oh, no, I'm bad, I'm bad, but not this, not this!"

"Go, then," I said to Arch. "Get."

"Pitt!" he shouted. "Go on down the trail!"

"Hell, no!" came back the answer in that voice of hideous tone. "I'm killin' that Dutch son of a bitch!"

"Hey you!" I shouted right back at him. "I'll kill *you* for talking rough to me in front of my wife!"

The encounter was a standoff. I couldn't get at him, nor he at me.

"Look, Dutchy," Arch said, as he bit the end off a cigar. "Pitt is comin' with us. You let him alone or there'll be bad things happen."

"Get him and go," I said.

Arch went on down the trail and called to Pitt, promising I wouldn't fire. After a minute, damned if Mackeson didn't come clean onto the trail about fifty feet away. He had holstered his pistol and was snorting like he'd heard a whale of a joke. These boys wore death like a garnish; it had no terror for them, and that scared me.

I walked out beside Turner and watched Mackeson close, but I didn't want to fight anymore. That is what it was, I just didn't want to fight Americans or Yanks or rebs or niggers or Dutchmen or nothing no more. Then that skunk hooted me, in full view of my woman. My trigger finger itched, but I still didn't shoot him and I knew I wasn't the same way I used to was.

Arch and Pitt loped away, not too fast.

"See oo, Yake," Turner said.

"Aw, no, Turner. Don't."

He wouldn't look at me. I couldn't get him to do it. His mind was set, and he shook his head and rode slowly away.

"Turner, Turner," I said. I walked fast beside him. "Damn it, man, come down our way with us."

All the response I got was him slamming in the spurs and galloping off.

I went to my wife and the baby Grace, and pulled them close to me. I cried with relief from not having been plucked from them. I had things to lose now, and that makes fearlessness a vice.

"Oh, Sue Lee," I said, and squeezed and squeezed.

Holt packed us up while I lingered in the hug, and when we were calmed it was on down the trail for us, and quick. I didn't want to hear the shots from Newport.

All that day, and for many days to come, we trotted muddy miles, through a war-sad state and a beautiful country. I knew it to my bones that my world had shifted, as it always shifts, and that a better orbit had taken hold of me.

I had us steered toward a new place to live, and we went for it, this brood of mine and my dark comrade, Holt. This new spot for life might be but a short journey as a winged creature covers it, that is often said, but, oh, Lord, as you know, I had not the wings, and it is a hot, hard ride by road.

DANIEL WOODRELL was born in the Missouri Ozarks, left school and enlisted in the marines at seventeen, received his bachelor's degree at twenty-seven, graduated from the Iowa Writers' Workshop, and spent a year on a Michener Fellowship. He is the author of nine works of fiction, including the novel *Winter's Bone,* the film adaptation of which won the Grand Jury Prize for best picture at the 2010 Sundance Film Festival and received five Academy Award nominations. *The Death of Sweet Mister* received the 2011 Clifton Fadiman Medal from the Center for Fiction, an award created "to honor a book that deserves renewed recognition and a wider readership." *Woe to Live On* was adapted into the Ang Lee film *Ride with the Devil.* His first collection of stories, *The Outlaw Album,* was published in 2011. Woodrell lives in the Ozarks near the Arkansas line with his wife, Katie Estill.

Reading Group Guide

WOE TO LIVE ON

A novel by

Daniel Woodrell

A CONVERSATION WITH
THE AUTHOR OF *WOE TO LIVE ON*

Daniel Woodrell talks with Matt Baker
of *The Oxford American*

Six hours into my drive I hit the Missouri Ozarks and Doyle Redmond's (narrator of Woodrell's novel *Give Us a Kiss*) description of the landscape flares up in my mind: "Our region, the Ozarks, was all carved by water. When the ice age shifted, the world was nothing but a flood. The run-off through the ages since had slashed valleys and ravines and dark hollows through the mountains.... These mountains are among the oldest on the planet, worn down now to nubby, stubborn knobs. Ozark mountains seem to hunker instead of tower, and they are plenty rugged but without much of the majestic left in them."

Daniel warned me that his house would be difficult to find, but I brushed off this warning, feeling confident that my car's navigation system would deliver me to his front door. But about a mile from his house my friendly navigation voice informed me that "turn-by-turn navigation" was no longer possible. I cursed and immediately pulled over because I realized I had no idea where I was or where I was going. I had a general map of the area but I couldn't pinpoint how to get to his house. I called my wife back in Chicago, and she pulled up a map on her computer and guided me, via phone, to his door.

He was outside, waving me down when I pulled up the small hill. I don't know if it was because I'd arrived ten minutes later than I said I would or if he knew that my directional confidence would be tested, but he seemed to realize that he needed to be out front, that I would probably drive by a dozen times if he wasn't. I was in the Ozarks, a little-known place that outsiders quickly stereotype and conveniently lob into the comedic punch lines, but a place, after all, that only natives can truly navigate.

This area (West Plains, Missouri) reminds me a little bit of Fayetteville, Arkansas.

Yes, especially this part of town where I live. We used to live in Arkansas—in Fayetteville, Eureka Springs, and in Jonesboro, for two semesters.

When you lived in Fayetteville did you run around with the University of Arkansas faculty and writers and such—Donald "Skip" Hays, Donald Harington, and others?

Yes, and speaking of Donald Harington, sometimes you get reviewed by someone who understands you so well that it really creeps you out. He was the first person to use the word "expressionism" to describe what I was doing. He was in his hospital bed when he wrote about *Winter's Bone*. His wife sent it to me, a copy of his handwritten review. He went out of his way for someone he could've regarded as a threat. Some people choose to see other writers from similar parts of the world as a problem and some of them don't. He was able to so thoroughly grasp what I was doing and even articulate it to me a little bit. I hadn't spoken to Donald in at least a decade. I knew Skip, and Dale Ray Phillips was around. And what I liked about Fayetteville is you could go down to Rogers Rec any afternoon and find at least one or two other writers hanging around, sometimes seven, eight, or ten of us. Skip would be there sometimes and he'd fill the table top with empty bottles, I do remember that.

I've heard that early in your career, agents and publishers were trying to direct you toward a strict genre style.

They were trying to. My first agent really felt that was the path for me. If you're writing, and not excited by it and getting some kind of interior pleasure out of it—that's difficult to explain to people who haven't experienced it—you really shouldn't do it. In terms of a moneymaking profession, you can find faster ways of making money.

Then you gravitated to writing about the great and mysterious Ozarks.

This region is just not really well defined in most people's minds. People don't understand that you can go out in the woods and run into some stained-glass artist from Long Beach. Eureka Springs has got two or three classical artists who have chosen to live there for one reason or another. I mean, you don't know what you'll run into out here.

(Katie Estill, Daniel's wife, walks into the room, and Daniel introduces us.)

You guys have been married how long?

Katie Estill: Awhile.
Daniel Woodrell: We've been married, uh....
KE: [Leaving the room.] Tell him in dog years.
DW: It'll be officially twenty-seven years in about a week. Been together thirty. We met pretty quickly at Iowa and followed each other. There seems to be a sense that you shouldn't hook up with another writer, but I think you have to have that talk at the beginning of the relationship: If you win, it's a victory for us; if I win, it's a victory for us.

You mentioned earlier that you think that the Ozarks are difficult to define. Why do you think that is?

One of the big problems for Ozark writers is the state line that separates it into Arkansas Ozarks and Missouri Ozarks. If we were all in one state I actually do think that would make some difference. And there might be one college or another—as in the case of the University of Mississippi, which is basically devoted to keeping Mississippi writers near the public and presented to the public, and their virtues are extolled by various symposia and whatnot. And, too, Faulkner being from

Mississippi, having an impressive town square that stayed alive and vibrant, and Square Books showed up, and *The Oxford American* was out of there a long time, and Willie Morris and all of these people who have been there one time or another.

And you think of Harington as representing the Arkansas version of the Ozarks.

I mention him all of the time. I'm just astonished how few people know who I'm talking about. And I don't know why that is. He's got the work.

You dropped out of high school, went into the marines, and then came back to Kansas City. Then what?

Yes, went back to KC and was only there a couple of months and went to Fort Hays State in Hays, Kansas, on the GI Bill, in-state tuition—

Much like Doyle Redmond in your book Give Us a Kiss.

Exactly. They had rodeos and all of that stuff. I'd never been in the cowboy world. Big ranches, and really big wheat operations, and big cattle operations, too. I'd never really lived anyplace like it—that flat—and I hated it at first, and then after six months I said, *It's gorgeous out here.* It just took me six months to realize it. I liked it very much, actually. I thought the people were great, very libertarian about everything. They didn't necessarily agree with my hippie ways, but they really just observed how you composed your-self and judged you on that.

In your novels I always sense a true respect for the readers, like you know they're right there, looking over your shoulder.

I'm always very well aware of the fact that I'm telling a story and I'm intending to keep you with me. The first time I ever had a story up at the Iowa workshop this girl says, "Don't you think it's sorta cheap to have an opening sentence that makes the reader want to keep reading?" That was my first class at Iowa and I'm thinking, *Oh, shit, what have I wandered into here?* I often think about bards, and I mention bards all of the time, because, by god, they had to tell a story that kept every class of person interested. There are probably a lot of dead bards, too, who wandered, went into lengthy labyrinthine digressions.

Yeah, they didn't make it.

Even Faulkner, at his most esoteric, is actually pushing the nar-rative. He is not languid. Sometimes he makes you confused, but he's not just lolling around, sniffing the lotus blossoms.

I don't think you get enough credit for your sense of humor. A book like Give Us a Kiss *made me laugh out loud. And even* The Death of Sweet Mister, *a very dark book, is filled with wonderful humor.*

I'm glad you say that because I think most of them have some of it in there. There are many people who say they don't see any of the humor. And some of the short stories that I've done are very macabre and dark. I remember Pinckney Benedict saying to me, after reading one of my short stories, "I don't know what you think of this, but I thought it was really funny." Hell yes, it was funny.

I'm sure you get bombarded with questions about the Ozarks from people who've never been to this part of the country. Do their questions ever come across as being extremely naive or silly?

They all want to know if the Ozarks I write about in my novels is what it's *really* like. No one has ever said that it's *all* like that. I mean, is everyone in New York a member of the gang in *GoodFellas*? I don't think so. People just want to believe that you're showing a total depiction, and also, it's almost like the idea of fiction is getting devalued. Everyone wants to know what's the truth of it. I'm getting a little bored with that question, because I never said I was anything other than a creative writer.

You incorporate many popular crime fiction themes into your novels and as a result you're considered a writer of crime fiction as opposed to a literary writer.

What we call crime fiction now, whether it's Lehane, Pelecanos, or Laura Lippman, essentially is social realist novels. And I completely agree with that. When I came out of Iowa, I knew that I never wanted to stand in front of a group of academics again and see if they wanted to hire me. I'm never going to do that again. So I would like to have one novel that had something you could take to the public. You don't need those colleges or academics to say you're groovy. You can just run right around them and take it to an actual reading public. So I knew I wanted elements of popular fiction in there to give me a chance to survive and develop.

Other than Winter's Bone, *which novel do people most often cite as their favorite?*

Tomato Red. It got some nice reviews but actually got far more nasty reviews than all of my other books combined. And most of them were from the South, which I couldn't figure out. I thought, *Is it the gay kid or what?* I don't know what it was.

Really? What did the negative reviews say? Why were they negative?

Oh, a variety of reasons. Some were mildly dismissive. Some were really ugly—one actually, I felt, went way beyond literary reviewing, and I asked my wife, "I didn't get drunk and fuck his girlfriend did I?" She said, "I don't think you did."

The Death of Sweet Mister *is my favorite. I still remember the chilling sensation I experienced reading the final line of that book, "I'd say no dawns ever did break right over her and me again."*

I actually felt like that book broke through in another direction. That was a case where once I got in the tune of it, nothing was in the way. And frankly, if I get in tune like that, if I'm not pulled out of it, I pretty much shuffle around in a robe staying in there. And I don't come out. That one was that way, and *Woe to Live On* was that way, too. I don't know what it is. I'm just running hard to keep up with it.

You wrote for quite a few years before garnering any recognition.

I wrote for ten years for nothing. And I wrote almost every day. I kept going because I liked doing it. If you really don't like doing it, it'll show up pretty soon. I filled up boxes of stuff that didn't go anywhere. But I needed to do that. And I don't think of myself as an incredibly fast learner. I learned at the pace that I learned at. But I'm told that ten years is about right. I had to emotionally develop. It's an emotional thing as well as a technical thing. And I had technique before I had the other. The emotional honesty is what really takes you further and further. It's an evolving thing.

You've always been a writer. You've never been employed in a regular job, not even as a teacher.

I was not equipped for the conventional world of employment and I didn't want to be—which has a lot to do with why I wasn't equipped. I just didn't want to do that. I would rather live under a fucking bridge and write on old grocery sacks if it comes to that. I remember once I was at a library and it was a place where all the homeless guys would come in and lay around all day and a guy from the university leaned over and said to me, "Dan, they all wanted to be writers once, too."

People make a lot about how you write about hillbillies, but most of your characters are not hillbillies, per se.

Nope, they're not. Most are just proletariat prone toward criminal activity. This house over here, nobody in that house has had a job in like three generations.

Did it take you some time to find your writing voice? Did it evolve or was there a moment when you felt like you achieved it?

At Iowa, a friend of mine and writer, Leigh Allison Wilson, was sitting around with Katie one day, laughing at a story I was telling them, and Leigh said, "How come you never do that in your fiction? Your fiction is cold and hard and stone-faced and chiseled. That isn't even who you are in your private life, you're so different from that." And Katie said, "You know what, that's true." That's a comment from a friend that ended up being very influential. I don't even think she knows how influential that ended up being.

The full, unedited version of this interview was originally published in June 2011 on the website of *The Oxford American* magazine (www.oxfordamerican .org), and is still available there. Reprinted with permission.

QUESTIONS AND TOPICS
FOR DISCUSSION

1. *Woe to Live On* gives a much different perspective of the Civil War than the clearer, more regimented North-South conflict in the East. What effect, if any, do you think these irregulars—both Union Jayhawkers and Confederate bushwhackers—had on the central conflict of the war? Would Jake and the other soldiers have been more effective fighting for the South with the regulars down in Arkansas?

2. In the first scene of the novel, Jake kills a boy in a manner that catches the attention even of the brutally violent bushwhackers: shooting him in the back as he attempts to free his father from hanging. What do you think were Jake's motivations? Pure ruthlessness? A desire to prove himself to the rest of the men? Or a strange version of frontier mercy?

3. Jake acts out of a more traditional sense of mercy when he works to spare Alf Bowden's life. But after news reaches the regiment that Alf killed Jake's father, it appears that Jack Bull is correct when he says, "You taught Alf mercy, but he forgot the lesson." Did Jake do the right thing, regardless of the outcome?

4. Jack Bull and Jake are peers on the battlefield, but in many ways they are very different men—particularly in their interactions with Sue Lee. Why do you think Jake is so tentative in his affections while Jack Bull is so forward with his? Why do you think Jake is so reluctant to take Sue Lee's hand in marriage at the end of the novel?

5. Jake tells Holt that "the rebel is a blight on the Yankee's will" and that the Northerners believe their "life and person have more loft" than the rebels'. For these men, what is the war about? Slavery? Territory? Or is it just a test of wills in which you are forced to pick one side or the other?

6. It's surprising to think of African-American soldiers fighting alongside Confederate troops, but Holt is loyal to the rebel cause. Why might that be the case? Is his connection to George Clyde strong enough to warrant such a decision, or is his affiliation just a product of circumstance?

7. How does Jake's German heritage influence his status with the rest of the regiment? With whom does it help him? With whom does it hurt him? Do you think that his position in the regiment would have changed if he were born to American parents?

8. Although somewhat reluctant to do so, Jake ultimately seems happy to have Sue Lee and the baby in his life by

the end of the novel. Do you think they'll make it to Texas? If so, is there hope for them to build a better life amid such strife?

9. The violence in *Woe to Live On* is swift, brutal, and omnipresent, but often Jake's narration treats atrocities as commonplace occurrences—just another man dead or homestead burned in a war of many. What effect do you think witnessing such routine horrors might have on a person's psyche? And what effect did Woodrell's understated treatment of the violence have on how you read the novel?

10. Much of *Woe to Live On* is based on actual history of the Civil War in Missouri and Kansas—Quantrill's raid on Lawrence was a real event, for example, and many characters, including Black John, Coleman Younger, and William Quantrill, are based on historical figures. How does the novel change your view of the Civil War and the men who fought in it? What elements of Woodrell's depiction of the war do you think are true-to-life? Which do you hope are fictionalized?